Velvet TIES

SUSIE CHARLES

Ellora's Cave®
Romantica® Publishing

What the critics are saying...

☙

"*Velvet Ties* started out as a suspense story and turned into one hot erotic read. [...] The author did a wonderful job of setting up the story for how the right answer just might be a trio, not a couple. I found the *Velvet Ties* to be a quick but very enjoyable read." ~ *Joyfully Reviewed*

An Ellora's Cave Romantica Publication

www.ellorascave.com

Velvet Ties

ISBN 9781419959325
ALL RIGHTS RESERVED.
Velvet Ties Copyright © 2007 Susie Charles
Edited by Raelene Gorlinsky.
Cover art by Syneca.

This book printed in the U.S.A. by Jasmine-Jade Enterprises, LLC.

Electronic book publication November 2007
Trade paperback publication October 2009

With the exception of quotes used in reviews, this book may not be reproduced or used in whole or in part by any means existing without written permission from the publisher, Ellora's Cave Publishing, Inc.® 1056 Home Avenue, Akron OH 44310-3502.

Warning: The unauthorized reproduction or distribution of this copyrighted work is illegal. Criminal copyright infringement, including infringement without monetary gain, is investigated by the FBI and is punishable by up to 5 years in federal prison and a fine of $250,000.
(http://www.fbi.gov/ipr/)

This book is a work of fiction and any resemblance to persons, living or dead, or places, events or locales is purely coincidental. The characters are productions of the author's imagination and used fictitiously.

VELVET TIES
ಬ

Dedication

To Mary, Debbie and Val
Much love to you for your encouragement and help –
and for holding my hand/giving me a boot up the creative
bum when I needed it.

Trademarks Acknowledgement

The author acknowledges the trademarked status and trademark owners of the following wordmarks mentioned in this work of fiction:

Babies 'R' Us: Geoffrey, Inc.
Honda: Honda Giken Kogyo Kabushiki Kaisha
Jockey: Jockey International, Inc.
Mercedes: Daimler Chrysler AG Corporation
Playboy: Playboy Enterprises International, Inc.
Prada: Prefel S.A. Corporation
Qantas: Qantas Airways Limited
Saab: Saab Automobile AB

Chapter One

"You have one new message," droned the answering machine.

Grateful for that small mercy, Melissa clicked the play button and waited for it to start, toeing off her high heels with a sigh of relief.

It wasn't often she gave herself the afternoon off, but with the end of the financial year accounting mess out of the way, she figured she'd earned it. And in celebration of her first half-year being such a rousing success, she'd even splurged on a very nice, very expensive bottle of red wine. Lifting her glass in a silent toast to herself, she poured a glass of Merlot and took a solid swig, allowing it to sit in her mouth, letting the flavors settle over her tongue and make whoopee with her taste buds. The effect was lost when the voice kicked in, and expensive red or not, it still burned a fiery path down her esophagus, her trachea and every other tube it shouldn't have gone down as she choked on it.

"G'day, sweetness."

Melissa froze.

"The game's over, Melissa. The wedding's all organized and it's time to come back home and assume your place. I've let you have your fun, so hand in your notice at whatever little job you're playing at because you're coming back with me..."

"*Let* me...?" she coughed out. "Little job?"

"I'm not taking no for an answer. And to make sure, I'm coming to London to get you, Mel... I'm sorry it's had to come to this, but you belong here. With me. And it's past time we made a start on Barry Junior. So start packing, honey, and I'll see you real soon."

Barry Junior? The answering machine clicked off, but Melissa's mind was already racing.

Well, fuck! How the bloody hell had he found her? Even her management company was in a corporate name. And her home phone number was unlisted.

"Dammit!" She should have known he'd never give up.

She took a couple of deep breaths, her mind spinning as she tried to formulate a plan.

Bugger it, she was through running. Her new life was in London, her business, her friends. She'd be stuffed if she was going to walk away from it all again. Barry needed to get the message they were over. *Finito.* No longer engaged.

So, what to do? How to ensure he got the message and caught the return flight to Sydney — without her?

It didn't take much to work it out. Not really. Barry Spencer wouldn't give up unless he knew, absolutely knew, there was no chance in hell of getting her back. Which left one solution. She needed to get married.

Married.

In one day, maybe two.

Crap.

Well, that wasn't going to happen.

But an engagement? That was a little more doable. The more she considered the idea, the more she thought it just might work. Of course, for that she needed a fiancé.

Okay, number one, she needed a man.

She paced the living room, tossing names around in her head, considering some, discarding others.

"Not just any man. He's gotta be big," she stated, and nodded to her image in the mirror over the fireplace. Barry was a big guy, not just tall but strong. Imposing. Whoever she chose had to be able to match good old Barry in that area at least. And he wasn't above using intimidation tactics. She'd seen him do it enough to know — personal experience not withstanding.

And someone wealthy. Barry and his brothers were rich as Midas in comparison to her.

"Shit," she ranted as she grabbed up the bottle and topped up her glass. That cancelled out half the potentials.

"Who then? Who? Who?"

Annoyed at sounding like a desperate owl, she raced into the kitchen to her handbag and grabbed her PDA. Scrolling through the names, she felt her panic rise once more as she discarded just about every name she found.

Socially and through her job, she knew lots of men. The thing was, the guy had to be prepared to go along with the ruse. Which meant, if she was going to convince Barry it was enough of a lost cause to hop on the next Qantas jet, she had to be prepared, at least once, to exchange body fluids with the guy. And there were some guys who really should stay friends — the platonic variety.

That left two names. One single. One married.

She'd try for single first. It was the easier option. Besides, she and Alex Ryan had a bit of unfinished business — especially in the exchanging body fluids department. Just thinking about him made her heart pitter-patter.

After leaving an urgent message on his mobile phone for him to call, she spent the next two hours wearing a track in her carpet, sweaty palm gripping her phone, waiting on him to call back.

At 7 p.m., desperation set in. She just didn't have any more time to waste. Hell, for all she knew, with Alex's business, he could be in downtown Timbuktu with no signal.

That left one name. So she'd have to draw the line at kissing with him. Just as well his gorgeous wife was a good mate. Maybe if Mel offered to baby-sit into the next millennium…

*****

Juggling the boxes and shopping bags in his arms, Thomas Danville closed the door on the old goods lift, and after a sharp jolt and shudder it began moving up. Behind him, his cousin Richard stumbled, regained his footing and breathed out a soft expletive, almost drowned out by the lift's laboring groan.

Thomas grinned. The lift might have been old, but it was the most direct route to the converted loft he and Elizabeth lived in over the old, converted warehouse. Considering the loads Richard and he were carrying, the fire stairs were not an option, unless they wanted to risk a hernia each.

Richard sighed, the sound tired rather than exasperated with the idiosyncrasies of the cantankerous old piece of engineering. "Thank God you two are only having twins," said Richard. "You should have taken out shares in Babies 'R' Us with all the stuff you've bought for these bubs."

"We could have brought it up in two loads, you know," suggested Thomas. "You were the one who wanted to get it all over with."

"Don't mind me." Richard Danville resettled the heavy box holding the second bassinette on his shoulder as it began to slip. "I'm just so blasted dry I can hardly spit."

The lift arrived at the loft, settling with a clank and another shudder. Thomas wrenched the door open then stepped aside in the open living area to allow his cousin to precede him down the hall.

"If you're grabbing a juice or something on your way back, Richard, could you get me one too?" Tom called out as his cousin sailed past him toward the nursery.

The phone rang. Thomas looked around, expecting the noise to bring Elizabeth waddling down the hall to answer it, but she didn't appear. Arms full of all the other baby items he'd purchased according to Elizabeth's "list", he pondered putting the lot of it down for a second to answer the phone but changed his mind. Easier to let the answering machine take it. If it were important, he'd make a quick trip to unload in the nursery, then come back and return the call.

"Tom? Honey...sweetie-pie...super-stud..."

Tom's face split into a wide grin at the cajoling tone of Melissa's voice coming through the answering machine. When her Aussie accent developed that sugary-sweet sound, he just knew it meant some major sucking-up was about to follow. He heard the refrigerator door open, the clink of glasses and the sound of Richard's footsteps growing closer.

"Help! Barry phoned. He's found me, and he's on his way here! And...well...I need a man." Melissa's soft chuckle filtered through. "Yeah, yeah, I heard that laugh, you rat! But it's only for two days — three, max! Please, I've told you what he's like. If you love me, you've gotta help. And I promise to baby-sit for you and Lizzy. Just call me Melly Poppins. Anytime. I'll be your on-call nanny. Just pretend you're hopelessly devoted until he gets the message and heads back home. I'm cute and loveable — you know that — so it shouldn't be too hard..." Soft laughter followed but petered out, the voice softening, "I'll owe you two — big time. Call me...please..."

Tom's mouth rose into a knowing smile. He took the glass from a frowning Richard. At his wife Elizabeth's recommendation, he'd hired her friend Melissa as his business manager the previous year, and the successful working relationship had developed into a very close friendship — one that surprised him. Melissa was a typical Australian — no airs or graces, brash, called a spade a spade, but she had an absolute heart of gold and that fact endeared her to him more than anything. However, his mother, the current Lady Danville and arbiter of all things "proper and refined", considered her coarse and vulgar, and refused to "sully" herself by visiting anymore if she knew Melissa was there. Which had been a major blessing. Elizabeth had asked Mel more than once to move in based on that fact alone. Especially since his mother still hadn't accepted his and Elizabeth's marriage—even four years later. And while he knew his generous wife would be more than happy for him to help out Melissa, he didn't want to be anywhere that would take him away from Elizabeth. With barely two months left of her pregnancy, and with twins on the way, she could go into labor at any minute.

A wicked thought came to mind. Picking up the phone, he dialed Melissa's number, his grin broadening as he waited for her to pick up. No answer. After a few rings, her answering machine cut in, asking him to leave a message.

"Melissa? Tom. Sorry, love. I'd really like to help, but the timing is terrible. Elizabeth's too close to delivering and I feel I need to be here. But I'm sure Richard would be thrilled to help."

Tom glanced up at the furious slashing motion Richard was making across his throat and just nodded.

"So I'll tell him to give you a call and the two of you can work something out. Must run."

He dropped the phone into the cradle and waited for the click, then ignored the danger signs on Richard's face and instead turned to smile at a still sleepy-looking Elizabeth as she shuffled down the hall from their bedroom.

"Hello, sweetheart," he said, wrapping his arms around his wife, rubbing a hand over her swollen belly. "Nice rest?"

She nodded and turned her head around to him, and he leaned over to give her a deep kiss.

"Hello, sweetpea." Richard's glare softened for a moment into a fond smile as he reached over to give Elizabeth a kiss on the cheek then resumed his stance with hands on his hips. "But what the hell are you doing, Tom? You know Melissa drives me nuts! She's...she's..."

"Gorgeous? Sexy? Spirited?" offered Elizabeth with a cheeky smile.

"In case you haven't noticed, she thinks I'm an arrogant prick—" Richard broke off and tossed a "Sorry, love" apology at Elizabeth. "She thinks I'm a total wanker. What *were* you thinking?"

"What I was thinking," Tom replied, straight-faced, "was that you two go together perfectly. Don't they, sweetheart?" Elizabeth nodded her head vigorously in agreement. "Never could figure out what went wrong between you."

"Me neither," agreed Elizabeth.

Richard's face hardened. "That's private."

"She'll help you get over..." Elizabeth tapped her chin thoughtfully. "The plastic blonde...what was her name, Tom?"

"Jasmine," cut in Richard. "And she was not 'plastic'."

"Yes, *Princess* Jasmine." Elizabeth grimaced. "Sorry, not plastic. Silicone. But heavens, what a bitch. Talk about stuck-up!"

"The word is 'refined', Lizzy love. Something your sweet Melissa knows very little about," Richard grumbled.

"I never knew you were such a snob, Richard," Elizabeth needled. "And anyway, it won't hurt. Just what the doctor ordered, if you ask me. You've lost your zing lately. Besides, Mel is such great fun to be around. You know she still has that teddy bear you won for her at the show." Lizzy chuckled. "Sits in a place of honor on her bed."

Richard's lip curled. "Oh, I'm sure. And she calls it Richard and sticks nasty-looking pins in it."

Elizabeth ignored him and turned to look up at Tom. "Remember when Mel was dating Leyton? She certainly knocked that stiff upper lip off him. I've never seen him so relaxed or having such a good time."

"And he couldn't keep his hands off her," offered Tom, sneaking a glance at his cousin's darkening visage. "There was this one time we caught him with Melissa in the—"

The shrill ring of the phone cut into their conversation. A quick glance at the caller ID let Tom know things were about to get very interesting. He let the phone ring.

"As I was saying, we caught Leyton and Mel—"

"I don't give a rat's arse what Melissa and that aristocratic pansy were doing. Aren't you going to answer that?" snapped Richard.

"Ah, no. I think I'll let the machine take it."

Turning away, Tom wrapped his arm around Elizabeth and winked at her as he steered her toward the leather sofa in the living room of their loft apartment. Just then an irate voice yelled through the speaker of the answering machine.

"Tom! Tom, pick up the damn phone! Look, do not try to fix me up with that cocky, arrogant twit! Mr. Richard I-wanna-be-Casanova thinks—thinks—he's every woman's dream! I mean, please! You've heard of 'eats, shoots and leaves'? Tom? Tell me you're joking. You're not, are you...shit! You are in so much trouble, Thomas Danville. Just you wait..."

One look at Richard, and Tom and Elizabeth burst out laughing. "You're right—sounds like Melissa isn't too thrilled about you. What did you do to her?"

Richard was glaring at the phone as though the woman in question were sitting on the desk. "Eats, shoots and *leaves*?" he spat, and spun around. "Why, that smart-mouthed little vixen."

"Yes, that's our Melissa," said Elizabeth. "But she's lovable underneath, Richard."

"Really? Well let's see, shall we? I think I'll go around there and let her know I'd be thrilled to partner her for her Barry's visit. Melissa won't know what bloody well hit her."

A feeling of unease niggled at Tom. He couldn't remember seeing his normally laidback cousin quite so irate. "Look, Richard, you wouldn't do anything to embarrass her, would you? I mean, she'd kill both of us."

Richard's eyes glinted with mischief as his hands landed on his hips. "First and foremost, I'm a gentleman, Tom. I would never embarrass a lady in public. Even one who holds dubious claim to the title. But there's more than one way to skin a cat. Especially this one. Now tell me about this Barry character."

"Well, we don't know all of it, but..."

* * * * *

Tom propped himself against the armrest on the sofa and made Elizabeth comfortable between his legs, leaning her back against him. His hand slipped up under the loosely woven sweater and caressed circles over her distended stomach. He chuckled when one of the twins kicked at his hand, and then a second time when his hand moved lower. "Those two are active tonight. You feeling okay, sweetheart?"

"Sure, I'm fine." She rubbed absently at the top of her belly. "Why?"

"You're very quiet. What are you thinking about?"

"Richard. He's so blind, Tom. And so's Melissa for that matter."

"The attraction between them?"

"Why can't they see it? Everybody else can."

Tom nodded. "I think Richard's in denial. He's hot as hell for her but from what I've been able to glean, Melissa's the first woman in a long time not to drop at his feet in adoration."

"She's been sweet on Richard from the moment she saw him, you know."

"So why the pretending she can't stand him?"

"I'm not sure—she's never said. But something happened between them, that's for certain. And they're both being very tightlipped about it—Mel closes up tighter than a drum whenever I mention him. Maybe it's that whole love-hate thing. Personally, I'd love to know what was with that Casanova comment."

Tom snorted. "This is Richard. It seems like he's been on a mission to sleep with half the female population of London since the day he got out of the SAS."

Elizabeth sighed. "I know one thing though—in spite of the 'career woman' image, Mel really wants what you and I have, Tom—a happy marriage to a man who loves and respects her and accepts her for who she is. I wonder if that's where Barry blew it? And you have to admit that Richard, as loveable as he is, is not the best candidate for a long-term relationship. So I guess she'd rather do without than settle for being on Richard's list of revolving-door women."

"So what do we do?"

"Nothing," she said, and laughed. "I think you've done more than enough, Mr. Danville. Did you see Richard's face when you mentioned Leyton?"

"Jealousy, thy name is Richard. He's got his work cut out for him though." A wide grin creased Tom's face. "But..."

Elizabeth turned slightly to face him. "But?"

"Did you see the twinkle in his eye just before he left? I think poor Melissa is about to be hit with a mega-dose of Richard charm."

"Hmm...what woman could resist?"

"You did."

She curled around and snuggled sideways against him as his arms tightened around her. "Yes, but I had you."

"You certainly did. From the first time I laid eyes on you."

"Ditto."

* * * * *

Melissa cursed as the vacuum cleaner snagged on something under her bed, the motor screaming as its suction became blocked. She yanked it back out and let out a "You stupid fucking idiot!"—not sure whether she was referring to the machine or herself—as she tried to retrieve a lacy pair of panties from becoming vacuum fodder.

Tugging and pulling at the delicate fabric didn't free it. She finally got a clue and turned the machine off. The item of underwear dropped onto the floor, looking as if it had been in a tug of war with a Rottweiler. It was then she realized she was panting from the exertion. She plopped down on the edge of the bed while she regained her breath.

Okay, so maybe she'd been overdoing it a bit. Cleaning when she was agitated normally relaxed her. Now she felt about as frazzled as a Desperate Housewife.

"Get a grip, girl!" she admonished. But dire thoughts of facing off against Barry on her own tugged at her. *No,* she reminded herself for the umpteenth time since she'd received the call, *you can do this. You're independent, strong, you're a modern woman. You can stand on your own!*

She fingered the braided panties in her hand and felt despondency settle over her like a cloak.

Anyone but Barry and she'd be fine. It was true—to most people she came across as confident, assured, a woman in charge of her own destiny and loving it.

Sure, she wanted marriage. She was a normal woman with everyday dreams—with the right man. Barry, she knew, was *not* that man. Her friends back in Oz all thought she was nuts, but then they hadn't lived with him.

She flicked back in her mind to the early days... At first he'd appeared to be the answer to every romantic dream she'd ever had—tall, sexy-looking. He'd swept her off her feet by the first kiss.

That was until she had a peek into life as a Spencer wife when she moved to Sydney from Townsville after their engagement and into the "little house" Barry called his "digs". *Digs.* Her entire apartment back then could have fit into the entry hall.

But that peek had been an eye opener—in more ways than one. What was it they said about never really getting to know a man until you lived with him?

Amen to that!

Leaving the cap off the toothpaste or leaving the toilet seat up... Hell, that was nothing. *That* stuff she could have lived with. What she couldn't live with was big. Much bigger than being swallowed up by a seatless toilet in the middle of the night because she was too sleepy to turn on the light.

She hit the cord rewind button on the vacuum with her foot and absently watched the vacuum suck up the cord then the plug until it jammed in so tight she'd need a screwdriver to free it next time.

She flopped back on the bed. Barry... What a mess she'd gotten herself into. Maybe she'd been naïve, a little too innocent. Definitely too innocent, she reminded herself.

Most women would have freaked out when they met his brothers—all four of them. All the same. It was the old "barefoot and pregnant in the kitchen" thing—between the four of them, they had twenty-two kids—so far.

But Barry had taken it to a whole other dimension. There was a difference between loving support and ownership. The "ownership" had started the moment he slipped that obscenely oversized rock masquerading as an engagement ring on her finger. As if it were the down payment on his investment.

First he started driving her to work, picking her up at night. Then it progressed to the half dozen or so phone calls through the day.

The constant nagging for her to give up her "little" job.

She loved her job! She was good at it, and she loved her independence.

Which had raised another issue—Barry Junior.

Now that they were *betrothed*—who the hell used that word nowadays?—there would be no more Pill, and there went her little tablets of sanity, flushed down the toilet, and the prescription for refills that went with them.

Motherhood was fine—someday. She just wanted *some* input as to when. Was that too much to ask? No, when Melissa married, it would be to a man who was prepared to treat her as an equal, not some brainless nitwit who was nothing more than a well-dressed womb and vagina.

A trip to the doctor for a nifty little implant had followed. As well as a hurried trip out the door into her own apartment until Barry cooled down and came to his senses.

Which he had a month later. Or seemed to.

Loving. Attentive. Romantic as all get out. And she'd melted.

Stupid, stupid, stupid!

Moving back in was a mistake.

The constant phone calls at work began again. The impromptu lunches.

Her girlfriends thought he was so sweet. She, on the other hand, felt smothered. Choking.

The limit was her boss calling her into the office to let her know they wouldn't be renewing her contract, since she was getting married to such a *wonderful*, loving man.

Barry. Again.

Even being unemployed hadn't been enough for Barry.

The phone calls stepped up. And then the insinuations.

Where was she? What was she doing? Who was she with?

So she'd met up with her old roomie from her university days. So he'd been a he. *So what?* It wasn't as if she'd climbed into his pants. Although hearing Barry rant, a person would think she'd had the whole university football team poking into every available orifice.

It was the final straw.

The next day after he'd gone to work, she'd left him his ring on the bedside table, and cashed in as many of her assets as she could lay her hands on at short notice. The first plane to anywhere, as far away as possible, had been London. But apparently halfway around the world and nine months was neither enough distance nor enough time to deter Barry the

Obsessive Babymaker. She should have gone with her first instinct and disappeared to Outer Mongolia.

Damn, damn, damn.

She looked down at the torn lace in her hand. *Ah, fuck it.* She rolled it into a ball then walked into her bathroom to toss it in the wastebasket.

"You," she told herself in the mirror as she stripped off, "are just being a maudlin cow."

It wasn't as if Barry could haul her back to Sydney if she didn't want to go. There were laws against kidnapping.

Hell, no. She was in London and that's where she was staying. *Damn right!*

Ten minutes later, after a nice hot shower, she was feeling a little better and certainly a whole lot cleaner.

The determined buzz of the doorbell reached her.

Wonderful. Visitors. Just what she needed.

"Bugger off, whoever you are!"

Unless it was the dreamy hunk from next door needing a cup of sugar or, please God, someone to massage his seriously buff body, she was liable to bite the head off whoever had such lousy timing. The day just kept going from bad to worse.

Grabbing her terrycloth robe off the hook behind the door, she wrapped it around her dripping body, cinching the belt as she headed to the front door. She took a moment to release the tight clip from her hair so that it fell down her back in its usual unruly tumble of light brown waves.

Smile pasted on her face — just in case it was Mr. Dreamy — she opened the door. One look at Richard Danville's grinning visage and her smile dropped.

"Oh, it's you."

No hunky next-door neighbor. Well, pooh! And the last person on earth she wanted to see. She started to shut the door in Richard's face, but a big booted foot leading up to a very strong jean-clad thigh wedged in the way. Rolling her eyes, she opened the door again but blocked the entryway with her body.

"Melissa darling. Just who I wanted to see."

"Well, that makes one of us. You must be confused, Rich. The Society for Hopelessly Pathetic Brainless Bimbos is on the next block."

Richard laughed, a short, dry sound, but his gray eyes twinkled. "Cute. Very. But I get enough of those in my day job. I thought I'd try the 'intelligent but lacking in social charisma' variety for a bit."

Ouch, that hurt. "Lacking in social charisma, huh? Who am I to disappoint? Here's a suggestion—why don't you piss off." She tried to shut the door and banged it up against his booted foot again.

He put his hand on the door and pushed it, the sheer bulk of his body moving into her personal space forcing her to take a step backward with it. "Look, now that we have the knives out of the way... You know why I'm here, Melissa."

"Seriously? No. Unless you're lost, in which case allow me to tell you where to go." She smiled sweetly at him.

His eyes grazed slowly over her, setting up a series of unstoppable flurries in nerve endings all over her body. When his eyes landed on her lips, the look was so heated her heart began to pound. Damn man. She'd forgotten the power of that look. Every single time he did it, her body began a nuclear meltdown. Hers and every other female's on the blasted planet. And she refused to be another piece of feminine fallout in Richard Danville's universe.

A single finger reached out and traced a line over her bottom lip, and it took all her self-control not to lick it.

His smile grew as his eyes darkened. "Careful, puss. All that sarcasm is really turning me on."

"Ooh, lucky me. Don't I feel special?" Once even his pet name for her would have sent her all aflutter. She refused to give substance to the little pitter-patter of her heart. It was probably indigestion.

Richard straightened from his slouch against the doorjamb, but with one hand on the door and the other on the doorframe, Melissa blocked his forward movement. That smile heated a little more, showing a flash of even, white teeth, and lit his eyes with a sparkle that could only bode badly for her.

There was no missing the way his gray eyes darkened as they left her mouth and dropped to her chest. "Oh, now there's a temptation if ever I've seen one. I'd forgotten just how juicy those little berries are."

She looked down and noticed her robe gaping, showing her cleavage and one perky, darkened nipple. "Well, you of all people know what it's like, Rich—you've seen one berry, you've seen 'em all."

"Trust me, puss, some berries were definitely not created equal. And darling, yours are a particularly delectable mouthful."

Considering he worked as personal trainer to—*and dated and bedded*—a predominantly female clientele who were, in the majority, built like professional triathletes with barely a B-cup between them, her generous Cs must have been a rarity. His look was so transfixed, the temptation was strong to flash him the other one as well, just to watch the reaction. It was hard, but she resisted the urge. Instead she pulled her robe closed, cutting off his view. "Isn't there some place you need to be? Some woman you need to annoy...I mean, sweep off her feet?"

He bowed low and when he rose, his head with all that soft, wavy hair almost skimmed the tips of her nipples, making her body shiver and her breath catch. He must have moved closer because by then they were eyeball to eyeball, their lips barely a breath apart.

"Your knight in shining armor, milady. At your service."

"And your trusty love lance too, no doubt. Tom sent you, didn't he?"

"When I heard the admiration in your voice as you talked about me, I couldn't help but offer."

"You heard?"

Richard nodded, a wry smile on his lips. "That's all right—I probably deserved it."

Melissa nearly choked on his words. "Well, gee, don't go apologizing—I'd hate to have to change my opinion of you. I just want to know why."

"I want to help."

"No."

Somehow he managed to look crestfallen. Her best bet was his knightly armor didn't get dented too often. "You mean you don't want to hear my proposition?"

"Does it involve you moving to The Falklands or something?"

"No. Better than that."

She smiled. "You're reenlisting?"

"That's what I like about you, Melissa darling. All that sass." A finger traced up the valley of her cleavage, lingered, swirled over her skin, tracing lines that were a touch away from a caress that had her heart racing. "But you need to drop the charade, puss. I know you're hot for me. I can feel it. Smell it. And I'm here to make all your wildest dreams come true."

Annoying her to the extreme, her traitorous skin goose-bumped along the path his finger had taken. The two biggest goose bumps were her nipples. A fact that wasn't lost on Richard judging by the interested lift of his eyebrow.

"You're delusional. All that female adoration has fried your brain. Some of us are a bit more discerning, you know."

He wrapped an arm around her waist and yanked her close so their bodies touched on every plane between their knees and lips. So close, he smelled intoxicatingly male, and hormones all over her body had skipped the little happy dance and moved straight on to the salsa. It was pathetic. Whatever happened to mind over matter?

"Not you, though, Melissa my love. You were all over me like a rash from the moment we met. In fact, since that memorable night—what, six months ago?—we haven't been apart since. You just can't get enough of me."

He nibbled on her neck and she pushed against him, trying to get air to her laboring lungs—not to mention oxygen-starved brain. The only thing he was correct about was the memorable night bit. As for the rest… "You really have lost it. Did you brain yourself with a barbell or something?"

"And I can't get enough of you…" Richard fished around in his pocket then grabbed her left hand resting on his chest. Before she could stop him, he'd slipped a diamond ring onto her finger with enough carats to keep Bugs Bunny happy for a month. Her mouth dropped open.

"Now it's official. Can't have an engagement without a ring."

"But…but…"

"Don't panic, puss—it's a fake. Admittedly a very, very good one. But not part of the family jewels."

He must have realized what he said because he laughed. "Slip of the tongue. No smart crack necessary." Then he tipped her mouth closed with a finger, brushed a quick kiss over her lips and walked past her into her tiny flat. Disquiet filled her when she noticed the khaki-colored duffel he had hoisted over one shoulder.

Short of manhandling him back out the door—a battle he'd just love and she was guaranteed to lose—she admitted temporary defeat and closed the door. "You forgot to take your meds, didn't you?"

"Now, now, is that any way to treat your *fiancé*? We have to make this believable for Barry. I think my story sounds pretty good, don't you?"

"Richard—"

He turned to face her with that infuriating smile. "Now how about a proper kiss?"

She folded her arms. "You're nuts. I'm not kissing you."

"Come on, puss. I'm all yours."

"Oh, I'm sure. Do I look that desperate?"

His eyes lit up with silent mirth. "Actually, yes, you do. So, when does Barry 'the walking sperm bank' arrive?"

She blanched. Tom and his big mouth!

But just the thought of it sent a feeling of dread to her tummy, and she placed a hand over it to still the butterflies. "Soon. That's all I know. Maybe tomorrow afternoon."

He held her by the elbows. "Come on, this won't be so bad. I promise to be good." He waggled his eyebrows. "And in return for helping you out, I ask only one small payment in return."

"Payment?"

He turned away from her to look over the photos of her family she had lined up on her mantel. "Sure, nothing comes free. I scratch your back—"

"Yes, yes, I get it." Her eyes narrowed. "And that 'payment' would be?"

He spun around. "A weekend. When Barry is safely back in Australia. You, at my beck and call."

At his...? "No. No way."

Richard's grin was positively wicked. "Got your flight booked to Sydney then? I hear Barry doesn't like to take no for an answer."

"You're a bastard, you know that?"

He leaned an arm on the mantel, absently straightening a photo that was out of line with the others. "But loveable. Come on, Melissa, surely you remember how great we were together."

"Sure, we were fucking fantastic. Until you—"

She cut off that thought. Being called by another woman's name right at *that* moment by a guy she'd been totally crazy over wasn't a memory she revisited too often if she could help it. "Look, never mind. That's done. Over. I want to know why you're doing this, Rich. If Tom somehow forced you into it, don't worry—I'll find someone to help me out."

Richard turned back to her, his eyes narrowed, the laughter gone from them as they darkened from the usual light slate with gold flecks to a stormy gray. "Who, like *Leyton*?"

Melissa enjoyed the look on Richard's face. It felt good to score one against him. "Well, Leyton would have been preferable."

Except that he was too busy with Lady Annabelle Dunleavy, the society princess he'd up-traded her for. Good riddance.

"So where is Mr. Perfect in your hour of need?"

"Getting married, last I heard." To the exquisitely blue-blooded Annabelle. Hopefully the Dunleavy millions would keep him warm at night because it would be small recompense for putting up with a woman who sounded like a stuck pig when she laughed and had a rather embarrassing problem with flatulence. She wished Leyton every success—he was going to need it.

"I have other friends."

"I'm sure—that's why you called Tom, who is also *married*."

"Oh, fuck off. I have another friend. He's just...out of range right now."

"He married too?"

"No. Divorced." She resisted the childish urge to poke her tongue out at him.

"What's his name?"

"Who are you—MI5? Alex Ryan, if you must know." She glanced down as Richard's bag dropped on the floor with a *thump*. What did he have in there—a fifty-pound lead bowling ball?

"What's with the duffel, by the way? You *are* reenlisting! Oh, be still my beating heart."

He chucked her under the chin. "Silly puss. I'm moving in. Looks like Alex blew his chance, so you and I will have to put on a good show for Barry instead."

She brushed his hand away. "Stop calling me 'puss'." His use of the nickname he'd gifted her with niggled. It was symbolic of better days with Richard before she'd found out what a total twerp he could be. "Define 'good show'."

"Like I told you, we've been inseparable since the moment we met. Madly in love. I proposed. We moved in together."

There was a catch here—she was just having trouble seeing it. "O-*kay*. But no funny stuff."

"Define 'funny'."

When she shot him a glare, he sidled closer. "We won't fool Barry if we don't kiss."

"I guess so," she agreed haltingly.

"And touching…we are meant to be in love."

Touching? Well, hell. "*Clothed* touching. Nothing…weird."

"And sex?"

Even though his face was expressionless, she had the distinct feeling Richard was laughing at her. "With you? That comes under the heading of weird," she deadpanned.

"Hmmm…we may need to work on that."

"No need. I've been there, remember?"

"Kinky and weird are not the same thing. I could prove it to you…"

"Thanks, I'll pass."

Catching her by surprise, he pulled her close, putting her arms around his neck before his slipped lower to band around her waist so they touched on every plane between chests and knees. She squelched the little shiver of delight as her hips cradled his erection. God, did he ever leave home without it?

"So, puss, touching and kissing."

She sighed. He was right—Barry would have a hard time swallowing the "madly in love" line if they didn't even touch.

"I guess so."

"Good. Let's start practicing..."

Chapter Two
ಬ

Richard was still mentally reeling from the revelation that Melissa knew Alex. It just made the whole thing even more perfect. Thoughts of what to do with Melissa during his weekend with her once Barry was gone were running over in his head. Kinky? Oh, his puss had no idea. And with Alex's help... Hmmm...a Melissa sandwich. It made him hungry just thinking about it.

She could bite and snap at him all she wanted, but Richard knew how much of the blustery show Melissa put on for everyone was just that—show. And if truth be told, he'd expected her to slam the door in his face. So the fact that he was in her living room with her arms around his neck, ready to pick up where they'd left off a couple of months previously was more progress than he'd expected quite so soon. Apart from the testiness she'd shown when he first arrived, she'd been cheeky, but all told, she'd been a pretty good sport.

That aside, Melissa was as skittish as a new foal. Testing his burgeoning theory, he ran a hand up her arm. She stiffened at his touch, but when her arms stayed linked around his neck, he persevered.

"You're going to have to stop flinching when I touch you if you want to convince big, old Barry that we're more than just friends." He breathed on her neck and relished the little shiver that ran down her back. "Aussie men don't touch their women?"

"Of course they do. And since Barry's so big on making babies, it's a bit hard to do that and not touch, you know?"

"Yes, I get the picture." A shaft of unreasonable jealousy burned through Richard. It was such an unfamiliar feeling that he was momentarily taken aback and pushed it away before he responded. "Well then, he'll find it odd if we don't touch, won't he?"

"I guess so."

"And especially if we don't kiss."

"Richard—"

"Come on, Melissa. We don't have much time to make this look natural."

As his mouth moved closer to hers, he noticed her breathing accelerate. Just a little. And only because he could feel the rapid flutter of her warm breath against his mouth.

And those tits. He could feel the hard tips rubbing against his chest through his T-shirt. He'd forgotten how good she felt up against him. He didn't date too many women who were nearly as tall as he, but every inch of Melissa's five foot eleven fit up against him like the missing pieces of a puzzle.

And lush. All curves and yielding flesh when he was used to muscles and tight everything. His other hand slipped lower to smooth over a delightfully feminine buttock that swelled out in a way that had his cock coming to rigid attention between one breath and the next. But then she'd always had that effect on him.

With a small amount pressure on her buttock cheek, he pulled her closer until their groins met. The fact that her legs were parted a little was perfect. Where they joined was all softness and heat. The most delicious warmth covered the stiff bulge in his jeans.

The scent of warm, wet, clean woman washed over him. Who would have thought he'd find the scent of soap so arousing? Interesting. And she tasted as good as she smelled. He had every intention of sampling the whole bloody smorgasbord, not just the appetizer she thought he was getting.

A finger against his lips stopped him before he could swoop in for the kill.

"You have had your shots, haven't you?"

"Shots?" he mumbled against her finger before he opened his mouth and sucked it inside.

A sharp, indrawn breath let him know he'd hit the mark.

"Uh-huh. Rabies, distemper..."

Laughter burst out of him. In retaliation he nipped the tip of her finger. "Wench!"

She tried to keep a straight face, but ended up laughing with him. "Well, a girl needs to make sure..."

"I'll give you sure!"

He caught her while she was laughing, grasped her head between his hands and pressed his lips against hers. He was going to take it easy. Seduce her. Take her unawares. Batter at her defenses with his slow, sensual assault until they crumbled.

Until the moment she softened against him.

Fucking hell!

A lot of guys underrated the power of a kiss, as though it were the most direct route to "Go". Not him. And never, ever with Melissa. The woman put her entire body into it—and there wasn't a man alive who wouldn't immediately envisage the two of them naked if he was on the receiving end. In his mind she was wrapped around him and his cock was already sliding into the heaven between her legs.

Her lips parted on a breath and the slide of her tongue against his—wetness and slick heat—was like his cock sliding into her cunt. The soft thrust and withdraw gave a whole new definition to oral sex. It was everything a kiss should be, everything he remembered—and if they kept at it, he was going to embarrass himself in a way he hadn't since he was an inexperienced, oversexed teenager. The woman had a mouth made for sin.

And just like that he was ready for her. Groins mashed together, rubbing against each other like cats in heat. He was two seconds away from taking her to the floor and fucking her brains out.

A lack of breath was all that pulled him up and he tipped his head back just enough to see her eyes. Lids still half-closed, she looked up at him, the green irises almost completely black. Lips rosy and swollen from the force of their kiss. When she licked her lips, leaving them glossy, and then hummed low in her throat, his cock started beating a distress signal in Morse Code.

Her arms slipped from around his neck, down his arms as she took a single step back, and he immediately missed the closeness of their bodies, the weight of her in his arms. "I guess you were right, Rich."

"About what?" Considering all the blood that normally kept his brain afloat was currently residing in his other, smaller head, he was suffering a severe case of short-term memory loss.

"I'd forgotten how good that part was."

"In that case…" he leaned in again to brush his lips over hers, slipping his tongue inside briefly before groaning low in his throat as he pulled away, "I'd say we're definitely even."

And it was definitely time for him to ease off a bit. He wasn't stupid enough to think Melissa wouldn't boot him out if she became uncomfortable, which is exactly what she'd be if he did what his body was craving—pulling her down to the rug and banging into her for all he was worth. *Smooth, Richard. So smooth…*

"Right." His voice sounded hoarse even to his ears, and he broke eye contact by picking up his duffel. "I'll just put this in your bedroom."

"Richard—"

He held his hand up, cutting off her words. "Barry won't think it's a little strange if I'm sleeping on the sofa?"

"Okay, fine!"

He swallowed a smile. His puss was rattled. Good. That made two of them.

He hoisted his duffel a little higher as he looked at the flush lingering on her face. It was ridiculous but it made him feel satisfied and possessive knowing he was the cause. "I'll put this away and be right back." He began to walk toward the bedroom.

"Richard?"

He turned at the bedroom door. "Yes?"

"This won't work if I have to contend with the Richard Danville Fan Club."

He sighed. He'd known it would come up. Better now than when Barry the Bozo was there.

"I promise. Cross my heart, Melissa. I'm all yours."

"Yeah, I've heard that one before. Just try to remember my name this time."

When a small frown creased her forehead, he was surprised that he wanted to move back to her and smooth it away — with his lips.

Christ, five minutes after achieving his first objective and it was already becoming way too intense. Another thing about them that obviously hadn't changed.

She cut into his thoughts. "I guess that means you've invited yourself to dinner?"

"We could order take-away. I'll pay."

Melissa rolled her eyes. "For a personal trainer, you have the most appalling diet, Rich. Look, I was going to cook for me. Easy enough to cook for one more."

"Awww, that's so sweet. You want to take care of me."

"Don't push it, rich boy."

Richard chuckled. "Want some help?"

"Of course. I'm not the hired help. I'll get started while you put your stuff away."

"Back in a sec."

"The bottom two drawers in the tall boy are empty if you need them," she said. "And grab whatever hanging space you need in the wardrobe."

"Thanks."

They stood looking awkwardly at each other for a moment. Then he turned into the bedroom before he did something odd, such as hugging her.

It only took a couple of minutes to put his things away. He took a perverse pleasure in putting his toiletries next to hers in the bathroom—as if a bastion had finally been breached. No man, that he knew of anyway, had ever stayed over at Melissa's, let alone moved in. The fact that he was the first, irrespective of the situation surrounding it, filled him with a smug sense of satisfaction. At that moment he felt like pounding his chest and hooting like a bloody caveman.

The delicious smell of lamb wafted down the hall as he approached the kitchen. He arrived in time to see Melissa turning some lamb chops.

"Lamb." He inhaled deeply. "God, that smells good. What can I do?"

"Can you peel the veggies?"

"That's it—give me the easy job."

"Well, I have to determine your skill level before I can let you go wild."

He moved up behind her and nuzzled her neck. "We still talking about the veggies, puss?"

She froze. Her eyelashes fluttered and he felt more than heard the quick intake of breath.

"Melissa?"

"It's just weird, Rich, all right?"

He picked the peeler up off the counter and grabbed a potato. Eyes on the vegetable when he'd much rather be watching Melissa, he carried on as if nothing unusual were happening. "I'm not sure if I should be offended. That's twice since I arrived you've used 'weird' and 'Rich' in the same breath."

"Well it is." After putting the chops back under the griller, she turned to face him and leaned back against the counter, arms folded across her chest. "We're standing here in my kitchen, getting dinner ready, and you're cuddling up to me like...like we're a couple or something."

"But that's good. The more natural it looks, the better Barry will be fooled."

"Yeah, I know, but still..."

She was right though. It felt so natural it was almost freaking him out. Richard put the peeled potatoes to the side and grabbed the head of cauliflower, looking at it. "How do you want this cut up?" he asked to distract himself from that disturbing line of thought.

He handed her the knife so she could cut off a few florets for him as a guide.

Out of the corner of his eye, he watched as she grabbed a saucepan, put butter into it to melt then scooped in flour and stirred.

"You're a good actor, Richard. That kiss before proves it—I doubt Barry will suspect a thing."

It wasn't just her words or the tone, but the implication that irritated him, and he put the knife down. "I'm not acting, Melissa. I never was with you. Good Lord, do you honestly think I'm that low?"

It was annoying talking to her back, but she kept her eyes on the saucepan. "It was pretty darn obvious you weren't really involved with me." She added milk and began stirring again.

"To *whom?*"

"Me. The 'fan club'. *'Ticia.*"

Melissa said the last word as if she'd just been force-fed a cockroach or something. Bloody Leticia. He could kick his own arse to Brunswick and back for the blunder he'd made on that score. The cardinal sin any guy learned as soon as he was old enough to know what to do with an erection — calling your current lady by the name of a past one in bed, even if there were extenuating circumstances.

"Not to mention, the last time I saw you, you were so rude, Richard!"

He gritted his teeth, remembering. "You were with Leyton at the tennis club, if I recall correctly." Seeing that smarmy prick with his paws all over Melissa the week after she walked out on him had been enough to make Richard want to shove Leyton's teeth down his throat. He'd come damn close. Leyton should have been happy he got off with a bit of messing up.

"The tennis set were greatly amused," Melissa said. "Stuck-up bunch of wankers. Your crowd already thinks I'm scum — like I give a shit."

"For starters, they're not 'my crowd' — "

"Tell that to Lord and Lady Stick-Up-Their-Arse." She turned to him with eyes flashing. "What I didn't appreciate was the very 'nice' talking to I was given by the president — it was 'suggested' that I avail myself of the public courts next time I get the urge for a game."

His eyebrows lowered in consternation. "But it was between Leyton and me."

"So?" she snorted as she added grated cheese into the sauce. "I was *obviously* the cause. As if you bloody toffs can do any wrong. All you little blue-bloods stick together. Can't have you cavorting with the convict element. You and Leyton are both part of the 'aristocracy', Richie darling, don't you know?"

With the atrocious upper-class accent Melissa affected, his name came out sounding like Ruchie, and a chuckle snuck out. "You're right — they are a bunch of wankers." He took the spoon out of her hand, pushed the saucepan off the heat and, gripping her shoulders, turned her to face him. "I'm sorry, Melissa. Sorry for what happened that night, sorry for…well, for everything. I screwed up."

Her eyes widened. "This is an apology? A real one?"

"Don't look so surprised."

"Do you mean it?"

"I do. Am I forgiven?"

Her eyes narrowed at him. "You're not just yanking my chain?"

"Give me a break, Melissa. I'm trying to do the right thing."

"Okay then. Forgiven."

"Love me?"

"Oh sure, give a guy an inch…"

He laughed. "Can't fault a man for trying."

"Yes, that's you—very trying."

"I'm not really that bad, am I?"

"We being honest?"

"I think it's about time, puss. Don't you?"

She swallowed. "Fine—honesty. I guess you're okay…" With a cheeky grin, she kissed him on the nose and eased out of his hold to get back to her sauce.

"Oh, that's generous."

"Only when you don't have the adoring flock interrupting every two seconds," she finished. She cast a glance at him over her shoulder. "Let's just say the man standing here in my kitchen helping me cook dinner is not the Richard I thought I knew."

"And you're definitely not the Melissa I thought I knew."

"No?"

"No, this one's much better."

"Thanks."

He gripped her waist and rested his chin on her shoulder. "And a fantastic kisser," he said, and blew in her ear.

She giggled. "Well, stick around. That's not the only thing I'm talented at."

"I know—trust me, I've never forgotten."

"Oh, you remember what a good cook I am?" They laughed together and she held out the spoon coated with a white sauce. "Taste."

He closed his lips over the spoon and his eyes drifted shut in rapture. Smooth with a subtle blending of delicate flavors that blossomed over his tongue—the slight tartness of the matured cheddar, a hint of…mustard perhaps and a spice he couldn't identify.

"Amazing. You are *very* talented."

"You better believe it."

He took the spoon out of her hand and dipped it into the sauce, coating it the same way she had for him. He raised the spoon to her lips. "Now you."

His groin tightened as her lips closed over it and she hummed low and long in her throat. He knew that sound. It was one he could hardly forget, since it had previously accompanied her swallowing his cock. Whether it was deliberate or not, and he suspected it was, the minx, it had the desired effect. His brain made the connection with his body and just like that he was harder than a totem pole.

"God, woman!" He stuck the spoon back in the pot and turned her around, grabbing her smiling face in his hands and kissing her hard, tasting the sauce on her tongue as he thrust his roughly into her mouth. She responded immediately, her hands moving to his chest, finding and caressing his nipples through his T-shirt until they puckered into tight discs.

His hands dropped to her hips, spanning the flare before his fingers dug in and he pulled her roughly against his leg, a palm sliding under her thigh to hitch her leg higher. He became so lost in the taste and feel of her, he was surprised, when she pushed away, to find they were still in the kitchen. They were both panting and she let out a little laugh.

"Um, okay, I think we've got the kissing part covered."

"Not quite. Maybe a few more…just to be sure."

"Cool down, Rich." She reached up and grabbed two glasses from the cabinet above his head. "Want some wine?"

"Can I drink it out of your belly button?"

"Richard!"

"How about—"

"No, you can have a glass like any normal person."

"Spoilsport."

* * * * *

Richard was feeling pleasantly stuffed. And mellow. Dinner had been delicious—and enough to feed half his old unit. The Cabernet surprisingly good, even out of a glass, and he was stretched out in bed—Melissa's bed—listening to her humming away in the bathroom while she cleaned her teeth and got ready for bed. Could life get any better?

Lizzy had been right—the teddy bear he gave Melissa was sitting propped up against the pillows on her bed, and the pleasure that discovery gave him had planted a silly grin on his face he still couldn't remove.

Just then the tap turned off.

He squeezed the soft bear as he looked at it. "Sorry, old son," he said to it before tossing it onto the chair beside the bed. "You're not needed tonight."

He folded his arms behind his head, a bigger grin spreading across his face as Melissa walked out of the bathroom. He wasn't much of a one for nightwear, but he instantly reassessed that thought if Melissa was the one filling it. With the light of the bathroom behind her for a heaven-sent moment before she switched it off, the shortie nightie may as well have been nonexistent. A certain part of his anatomy jumped to attention and saluted her choice of attire.

The grin turned smug at the priceless look on Melissa's face. Especially when her gaze zipped straight to the king-size erection currently doing a good impression of a divining rod the closer she moved to the bed.

She sighed and shook her head at him—or rather at his erection. "I told you before, Rich, no loaded weapons in the bed."

"That's okay—the safety's on. Unless you decide to pull the trigger." He laughed at her as she rolled her eyes. "Besides, it's my show of appreciation, puss. You're gorgeous. It's responding. Simple male mechanics."

"It's as big as a bloody bazooka and it's not coming to bed with us. Damn thing takes up half the space."

"Nice of you to notice." He waggled his eyebrows at her. "How about if I tuck it somewhere nice and warm?"

"Your armpit? Even yours won't reach that far, big boy. Lose it."

"How?"

"You're a clever guy. I'm sure you'll think of something." With a tipsy little giggle Melissa turned her back, pulled up the quilt and snuggled down—as far on her side of the bed as it was possible to get without ending up on the floor. With a reaching hand she turned off the light, plunging the room into darkness. "Sweet dreams."

Sweet dreams, his arse. Deflated mentally if not physically, Richard covered himself with the quilt and turned on his side to face Melissa's back. He could feel the warmth coming off her. He took his aching cock in hand, visions of sliding up against Melissa and nestling it in the crack of her buttocks, sliding through to her pussy, just making him ache more.

He'd hardly moved, thinking a little persuasion was all that was needed, maybe some dirty talk—Melissa loved that—when a soft snore began on the other side of the bed.

Well, damn.

Now what?

* * * * *

A soft hand was stroking his cock, teasing and torturing every hard, throbbing inch. And a mouth was nibbling and licking at his neck. Wet little nibbles that scored a path of fire up to his ear and sent flames through his blood to spark a riot of sensations that made his breath catch and his heart pound.

And the only thought that could form in the sensory overloaded synapses of his brain was *Don't stop!*

His hand was curved around a breast, the skin so silky soft, and the hard nipple just begging to be tweaked and plucked. He palmed the weight of it, his mouth watering to close around the nipple.

God, if he was dreaming, please don't let him wake up.

Closer. How could he get closer? It was warmth, it was heaven, and he wanted... Christ, he wanted to fuck so badly he felt as if he were going to explode.

And that mouth. Damn, he needed that mouth. On his cock. All that warmth and wetness sliding up and down his shaft.

But first...first he wanted to kiss it. He was starving for a taste. He'd never felt as if his sanity hinged on tasting a woman before, but something about this one...

All it took was to turn his head a little sideways and those soft lips brushed over his. A tongue swiping along his lips. He opened his mouth wider. Tongues met, rubbed and tangled. Slow, achingly erotic. As if every taste bud were exploding.

Skin touched skin, legs entwined, hands grasped, and he inhaled through his nostrils, unwilling to break the tight seam of their mouths. A familiar fragrance went straight to his head, making him needier, hungry for more. When a leg lifted over his, his hips pushed forward of their own volition, nestling their groins together. And every hard inch of his erection pointed at paradise. The head nudged and found what it was searching for. Pussy lips closed over the head of his cock and he held still, his body rigid from wanting to thrust and finish that silken slide into heaven. But this was a moment to be relished, not rushed. Nothing—absolutely nothing—ever surpassed this moment.

Small thrusts, her labia barely cresting over the ultrasensitive tip of his cock, sent waves of pleasure in continuous ripples from his shaft straight up his spine, making arms, legs and back tingle and clench in anticipation. The heavy sac of his testicles drew up tight against the base of his shaft when a flood of moisture slipped down over the flared crown of his erection.

A surprised cry destroyed the hazy sensual feast of the dream, pulling him from his erotic imaginings to instant alertness and the crystal clarity of reality.

Eyes blinked open. His heart pounded.

In the light of the full moon filtering into the bedroom through the sheer curtains, he could see Melissa looking at him. Eyes big as saucers. Lips a little puffy and wet. That kiss was no dream.

Neither, apparently, was what was happening lower down. Their bodies were frozen, still partially locked together.

And God, it was so fucking good. The feel of her. The taste of her that lingered on his tongue. He couldn't let her go. He knew he should, but his arms just refused to obey.

He wanted to say something—anything—but if he did, if he shattered the spell they were under, she'd move away, and he felt as if he'd die if she did. A heavy silence hung between them while they each absorbed what they were doing.

She saved him from saying the wrong thing by speaking herself. "You drunk?"

Her voice was a little breathy, nothing compared to the ragged croak he came out with. "No. Sober as a judge. You?"

"Same. I thought I was dreaming."

"I'm glad I'm not. Fuck, I want you."

"Bit late for that, don't you think?" she said, and blinked heavy, slumberous lids at him. The look on her face just turned him on more.

"Hate to waste it."

"You do and I'll have to hurt you," she gasped against his ear, the heated whisper of air over the sensitive lobe going directly to his cock, making it throb.

She was going to be the death of him. He should take his time. Make love to every inch of her. Show her how much he'd missed her—all of her. Until he felt a hand free itself from his neck and dig into his buttock.

He gritted his teeth, determined to hold back since a two-second fuck was *not* what he had in mind for the first time he had her horizontal again. His determination lasted until small teeth nibbled on his neck, up to his ear. Damn it, she knew his "on" button too well.

"I'm waiting, Richie."

He groaned even as his pelvis jerked, half burying him inside her. "Just so we're clear..." he plunged in further, gritting his teeth against the tight grip of her pussy around his shaft, "this won't be the only one tonight, Melissa. We have a lot...of time...to make up for." He withdrew again and growled at the feeling as he sank deep once more. "And I'm going to make you burn, make you scream for me."

Arms locked around his neck as she fought to hold on, she ground herself against him, burying him deeper with each rotation of her hips. "You really talk too much—"

Her words were cut off as he surged inside her then pulled out before driving into her to the hilt, the thrust punctuated by the sound of flesh smacking together.

Harder. Faster. A soft grunt left her mouth each time he thrust against her mound, rubbed against her clit. The sucking sounds of her juices each time he withdrew drove him crazy. Trickles of sweat ran down his back. He rolled over the rest of the way until she was underneath him, her ankles locked high on his back, raising her hips so every inch of him was swallowed in her channel.

"Kiss me. Damn it, Melissa, kiss me like you can't get enough of me."

Grasping his face, she pressed her lips to his. Her tongue rubbed and teased, a muffled moan escaping before she broke away, gasping and panting. Shudders began to move through her body and she threw her head back, her back arching off the bed. He dipped his head, taking a nipple into his mouth and tugged, pulling on it roughly the way he knew she loved.

"God, I can't stop it. I can't hold on, Rich."

Bloody hell. She was there. Just like that.

She started trembling, shaking, clamping the walls of her cunt around his cock. His name falling from her lips again and again.

It was too much. Tingles shot up through his balls to his shaft and, with a bellow and one deep thrust, he blasted inside her, his hips jerking with each explosive surge of semen. Coming and coming until his legs trembled and shook, and he had to brace an arm next to her head to prevent himself from falling on her.

"Well, fuck me," he panted, gulping in huge draughts of air to replace the oxygen that had been sucked out of his lungs.

He couldn't remember the last time he'd come so hard.

"I just…did," she chuckled between gasps, "but…maybe…we should…try it again. Practice…makes perfect."

His breaths still shuddering in his chest, he laved her nipple, panting against the damp skin, licking at the salty perspiration and feeling her shiver in his arms. "You have a wonderful mind, puss. Simply wonderful."

* * * * *

Outside the sky was starting to lighten.

The fact was peripheral except that, as he lay there propped on his elbow, the bit of light allowed Richard to watch Melissa as she slept beside him, the warmth of her back snuggled against his chest. His hand idly stroked the soft skin and full, rounded curve of her hip and buttock. To a lot of men, him included, she looked like a perfect vision of womanhood—lush, earthy. Until she opened her mouth—God only knew what was going to come out of it. Even her laugh was unreserved. But she had a face like a doll. Leaning over, he kissed the light smattering of freckles across her cheek. He was rather fond of those. Along with the dimples. He was especially fond of the dimples.

He should be getting up. Taking a shower. He had his first client at 6:30 but dragging himself away from Melissa long enough to get his head functioning was the problem. The minute she looked at him with that ravenous fire in her eyes all he could think of was fucking her.

Last night was a perfect example. That first one they'd stumbled into from sleep. But later she'd slipped her hot mouth over the head of his limp dick, drawing him from an exhausted sleep to an almost instant throbbing hardness while she laved and sucked, licked and nibbled. She hadn't given up until he roared loud enough to wake the whole bloody neighborhood as he pulsed into her mouth, holding her head as he jerked and jetted, even when he felt he couldn't possibly have anything more left to give.

Shit, just thinking about it made him hard as a rock again.

His arms tightened around her and his head dropped to nuzzle at her neck. He had a little more time...

Moving the long locks of silky hair, he scattered little kisses along the line of warm skin from her neck to her shoulder. Lifting her leg over his thigh, he nudged the tip of his erection against the still-damp folds of her cunt. He bit his lip as he slid slowly in, stifling a moan as the warmth of her pussy closed around him.

And just like that, he wanted her with an almost violent hunger that shook him to his core. And it shocked him to discover the edge of his need for her hadn't even been blunted through the night.

She was fiery, passionate, uninhibited — no wonder Barry was traveling halfway around the world to take her back home.

Slowly he started to stroke, reaching with a finger to lightly caress and circle the sensitive nub of her clit. He grinned when she mumbled and moaned softly but didn't wake, just pushed back against him. Sometime during the night he'd finally worn her out.

The orgasm built slowly, gathering momentum as she rocked against him in her sleep, the heat sucking him back in each time he withdrew. The slow tempo was an exquisite torture, the walls of her pussy scraping and caressing every inch of his cock.

He inhaled deeply, the faint remainder of her perfume, the scent of their lovemaking, imprinting it on his memory. When little whimpers escaped each time she breathed out and the walls of her cunt started to spasm around his cock, he fought to keep his thrusts gentle, feeling the electricity streaking down his spine, spreading, gathering in his balls, pulling them up tight. Fighting to hold on, conscious of the thickening of his shaft as he prepared to come, he pushed gently until he was buried deep, gritting his teeth as he held still and let the explosion overtake him in rolling waves.

His hips jerked. His cock throbbed, bathing her womb, come pulsing from the tip in long jets. He threw his head back and bit his lip to stop the howl that wanted to break free as indescribable pleasure flowed through his body.

Forehead resting on her shoulder, he stayed nestled inside her for long moments after, clasped in her heat and wetness as he softened before he withdrew, slipping easily from her. His cock was damp with their combined juices, the bed pungent with the smell of their lovemaking.

Now he really needed to be moving and get to work. But what a way to start the day... With an unfamiliar twinge of regret, he lifted the quilt and slid from the bed, taking care not to wake her as he tucked the quilt around the curve of her body, and padded to the bathroom.

* * * * *

Richard stood in the kitchen drinking a cup of Earl Grey, listening to the water from the shower running. And someone singing. Badly. Out of tune.

It was such a happy sound though, Richard wanted to smile.

But he couldn't. His feet planted on the floor, his entire body rigid, it was only with the greatest difficulty he remained at his position in the kitchen and didn't fling clothes off willy-nilly in a rush to get naked and join her in there. Just the image of all that lush flesh with soapy water sluicing over it was enough to give him the hard-on from hell.

He took another sip of tea, noticing the white-knuckled grip he had on the mug.

A hard-on that could just get the idea of more morning sex right out of its little one-track mind in its pea-brain head. Whatever warm, fuzzy feelings he still nurtured after their night together had been cruelly dashed after his shower when he went to wake her with a good-morning kiss.

Her offhand "You still here? Amazing…" had deflated his mood quicker than a balloon stabbed with a Swiss army knife.

Of course he was still there. Where the bloody hell did she expect him to be? Hell, he knew the answer to that. The "eats, shoots and leaves" comment still rankled. Twice he'd done that before. Twice. But damn it, he'd had to get to work. And what woman wanted to be woken up when it was still dark just so a guy could say goodbye?

So he was waiting for her to get out of the bloody shower just to make a point.

That wasn't what was bothering him the most though.

Still floating in the euphoria of dipping into a woman bareback for the first time since he was a teenager, it was the "you'd better not give me anything" crack that made him want to spank that cheeky bum she kept flashing at him until she couldn't sit down for a week. She made him sound like a communicable disease. Damn it, he was clean. And he was careful. At least until last night. *Shit.*

"That's better," the subject of his niggling annoyance sighed as she breezed into the kitchen, fresh as a daisy from her long shower—too bloody long for his overactive imagination—tying her silky robe in front. "Got one of those for me?" she asked, nodding at his cup.

"Kettle's hot. Look, you and I need to get something straight, Melissa."

She grabbed a mug from the cupboard and flicked the switch on the kettle. "Oh? What's that?"

He put down his mug and grabbed her, placing his hands on her waist. He gritted his teeth at the warmth her skin gave off.

"Rich?"

As his grip firmed, his hands sliding up over the silky fabric until they stopped just under the curve of her breasts, the green of her eyes deepened, her lashes drooping a little, and when she unconsciously swiped the tip of her tongue out to wet her lips, he heard the final threads of his control zing and they snapped.

"This."

Her eyes wide, she looked at him as if finally seeing the effect she had on him.

He yanked her against him, lowering his head, all his senses heightened, and drew in every little thing about her—the warmth of her body where his hands spanned her ribs, the scent of fresh lemons on her hair, her skin, the feel of her hands sliding around to the back of his neck.

When he touched her mouth, it was as if two months and a whole lifetime of need poured out of him. As his mouth moved over hers, his teeth nibbled the soft curves of her lips, his tongue licking along the partly open seam.

His arms wrapped around her so she was flush against him, so the thick ridge of his erection pushed against her soft belly. As she gasped, he thrust his tongue inside her mouth, feeling a surge of male satisfaction as the sound was replaced by a moan and her arms locked tighter around his neck.

Faster and faster, he moved restlessly over her lips, rubbing and twisting his tongue with hers, feeling it deep in his groin when she responded, their mouths mating furiously.

In his pants, his cock jerked against the metal teeth of the zipper. What he wouldn't give to feel her mouth swallowing his cock again—here in the kitchen—and watch those luscious lips stretch over the broad crown as he held her head and fucked her mouth, watching the shaft glisten with saliva each time he pulled out.

Hell. Forcing himself to back off, he pushed her away to arm's length. Taking a deep breath, he tightened his grip on her arms as he wrestled with his control.

"Barry or no Barry, I will not be your fuck-buddy, Melissa. Let's get that straight right now. What happened in there," he jerked his head in the direction of her bedroom, "was not casual sex. So don't fucking treat it like it was."

For once Mel looked speechless, which, Richard decided, was a good thing. He liked her that way. A smile of satisfaction formed on his face. *Now* he felt better. "So, what time do you want me home, honey?"

Chapter Three

Richard checked his watch as he walked out of the lift and strode the few steps to the door of *Fides*. It was the first time Richard had visited Alex's new offices. From the look of the place, Alex's international security business must be booming. Half a floor in an office block on Basinghall Street. Lots of steel, chrome and glass with a view half of London would kill for. Richard whistled softly.

He turned to the woman sitting at the large teak desk.

"Hello, Prue. Is the boss in?"

The stunning thirty-ish blonde turned coquettish, her eyes twinkling as she replied with a "Depends. What's it worth to you, gorgeous?" and smooched a kiss at him.

It was standard repartee between them, but as much as he tried to smile back at her, for some reason his face didn't want to respond. Prue flirting with him was just one of those things. Fun. Harmless. Even if he did know she wanted inside his jeans in a big way. As if that would ever happen. Cute as she was, there were some women who were hands-off — other men's wives, bosses and, as in this case, personal secretaries of best friends.

But today Prue's saucy innuendo felt like ten-inch nails raking down his back — not so pleasant. In fact, now that he thought about it, he'd been a bit "off" all day. Maybe he was coming down with something...

"Sorry, Prue honey, but this is kind of urgent. Does he have five minutes he can spare?"

He and Alex had trained and served together in the Army first, then the SAS, an experience that had bonded them closer than most blood relatives. *Best friends* didn't even cut it — if it came down to it, he'd take a bullet for Alex, and he knew the reverse applied. It was the reason why he knew, no matter how busy he was, Alex would see him—especially if it was urgent.

Prue looked a little flattened by his brush-off, but pasted on a professional smile. "Sure, just a second, Richard, and I'll check."

Prue rose from behind her desk and wiggled her way over to Alex's office door. It was a nice view, one Richard normally enjoyed, but today it left him feeling flat. Not at all interested.

He had to be sick. The lady had legs a man would kill to have wrapped around him.

He wandered over to the floor-to-ceiling windows and looked out at the impressive view of St. Paul's, scratching his head in confusion.

Or maybe he was just tired. He hadn't slept much. Lord, how could he—sharing a bed with Melissa. And not after they'd... He shook his head in resignation as he felt his cock responding to the memories, thickening and stiffening like it had a mind of its own. The minute her name entered his head, the damn thing was like a puppy dog sitting up on its haunches begging to be noticed. Pathetic...

"Richard? You okay, mate?"

The familiar baritone made him look around. Alex was standing in the doorway to his office, the huge bulk of his frame filling the narrow space.

Richard quickly shoved his hands in his pockets to disguise the burgeoning erection. "Yes, why?"

Not quickly enough, judging from the knowing glint he saw in Alex's eyes. "Just a feeling. Come in."

Alex turned and walked back into his office. Everything about him just screamed ex-military—the bearing, the short, neat haircut, the clothes immaculate. Maybe that was a big part of the reason why his security business was so successful.

There was a quiet but absolute confidence about the man that filled the air around him, that made his clients feel their safety was assured in his hands.

Richard followed, absently registering the click of the door as Prue closed it behind them.

"So," said Alex, taking a seat behind his expansive desk, "to what do I owe the pleasure? You look distracted, if you don't mind me saying. Prue seemed quite put out."

Richard rolled his eyes at that final comment. "She'll get over it. What I'm here about is a friend," he offered then added softly, "a very good friend." And realized as he said it, it was true. Whatever misunderstanding had occurred between Melissa and him before, there was still that same "fit" with them, a natural ease with each other that no amount of time could develop. "More importantly, a mutual friend."

Alex leaned back in his seat. "Plenty of those about. Male or female?"

"Female."

"With you, why am I not surprised?"

"It's Melissa...Melissa Blake."

Alex's entire body stilled and he closed his eyes for a moment, his only movement, and it spoke volumes to someone who knew him as well as Richard did.

"So it's true," said Richard. "You do know her." The look on Alex's face made him ask, "Have you fucked her?"

Alex's gaze turned steely. "Any man who fucks Melissa instead of making love to her doesn't deserve to share the same bed."

A small grin kicked up the corner of Richard's mouth. From the sounds of it Alex had been bitten by the same bug as he had. "You had a call from Melissa yesterday, yes?"

Alex nodded.

Richard took his seat finally and made himself comfortable. "I think you and I had better have a talk, Alexander."

"You mean *you* know why? Because from what I hear, she thought you were right up there with the Bubonic Plague."

"I charmed her into forgiving me — what can I say?"

"I say you're full of shit." Alex chuckled. "I've tried to call her back about half a dozen times today but she must have her mobile phone turned off."

"She has a...situation. Barry's on his way. You know who I'm talking about?"

The smile faded from Alex's face. "Melissa's ex. She left him about nine months ago and moved here."

"He's found her, Alex, and he wants her back. I'm acting as her new *live-in* fiancé to put him off the scent and send him back to where he came from — without her. If you'd answered your bloody phone, you might be in bed with her instead of me. Remind me to thank you for that someday."

"Melissa asked you to play her fiancé?"

"You find that so hard to believe?"

Alex just raised an eyebrow at him.

"Oh fine! So I sort of offered."

"Using that famous Danville charm, no doubt."

"She couldn't resist me."

Alex snorted. "I'll bet."

"How do you know her?" he asked Alex.

"I met Melissa about a month after she arrived here. She was the assistant to that puffed-up twit at the Aussie embassy for the Australia Day function. Talk about a security nightmare... It was about the time of those terror attacks on Heathrow. Everyone was on edge. Anyway, we had to confer quite a few times in the lead-up and then on the night. I got to know Melissa...very well." A smug grin crossed Alex's face. "We kept each other warm for about a month after that.

Ultimately, though, the timing was rotten—she'd just left Barry." Alex looked down briefly then raised eyes now darkened with shadows, a heavy frown creasing his brow. "And Cilla and I had not long divorced." Alex grimaced and Richard nodded in acknowledgement. Cilla had ensured, in her most vindictive manner—the spiteful cow—that the divorce was unpleasant. As their personal affairs were hung out for all and sundry to gawk over, it had been a tough time for all of them. "Not exactly the most propitious time for starting something serious for either Melissa or me," Alex reflected.

Then he nailed Richard with one of those no-nonsense looks. "Melissa's very special to me, Richard."

Richard nodded. "Good. So you won't mind looking into this Barry character for me?"

"For you. For Melissa. Consider it done." A small smile lightened Alex's face, chasing some of the shadows away. "She still looking good?"

"Every beautiful, luscious inch of her."

Alex's laugh was a short, sharp bark. "You should see your face. You've got it bad, mate."

"Not me. I know what I'm doing." He shrugged off Alex's comment. "So, what do you need to know about Barry?"

"Nothing. I did a brief check on him back when Melissa and I were seeing each other." Alex's eyes narrowed. Obviously he hadn't been happy with what he found out. "Let's just say, I know where he lives."

"I'd better get going then. I promised Melissa I wouldn't be late home in case Barry arrives tonight."

"You need me to help deal with Barry, just call. Anything. Any time—day or night."

"Count on it."

Richard grasped the doorknob then let it go when Alex spoke.

"If she's the one, Richard, you just say the word and I'm there."

Richard turned slowly. His gut clenched and he stiffened. He knew what Alex was talking about.

Sharing. One woman. On a permanent basis.

For different reasons, it was a need, a hunger they'd both shared since they came back from the Middle East that last time. A need they'd thought Cilla was the answer to. Before she married Alex. She wasn't. Instead, she'd played one against the other, trying to drive a wedge between them that had nearly succeeded until Richard left, moved back out on his own. No woman was worth losing their friendship over.

After what had been a torturous few years for Richard, the situation with Cilla had been the final straw. He'd made a decision after that not to leave himself open to that sort of pain ever again. He opened the door. "Call me when you have something," Richard tossed over his shoulder as he walked out and closed the door behind him.

After the door closed behind Richard, Alex spun his chair around until he looked out the window. Night was falling quickly and London was lighting up, the tarty display of flash and glitter like a whore at a Christmas party.

But Alex barely registered it.

Richard's reaction wasn't unexpected. No one knew better than Alex what he'd been through. But it was time to put that in the past. Move forward. What Richard needed was someone they could both love, protect. Who would be theirs. Love them back. Together.

A laughing pair of green eyes slipped into his mind. The softest body stretched out underneath him, hugging him. And the sweetest lips God had ever put on a woman.

Melissa.

* * * * *

The sun was just starting to set as Richard parked his Saab behind Melissa's brand new Honda.

Whistling, he walked up the path to the front door, paused his happy tune while he searched on his key ring for the house key Melissa had given him.

A perverse part of him was really looking forward to the coming confrontation with Barry. Plus, giving Melissa a bit of her own back would be too much fun.

As he went to insert the key, the door swung open. He frowned at that. What was she doing not locking the door?

Voices came from the kitchen. One Melissa's. The other one deep, male. Distinctive Australia accent.

If that was the infamous Barry Spencer, Richard was curious to see what sort of man Melissa would actually say "yes" to. He stepped through the living room toward the kitchen from where the voices emanated.

"No, Barry! Stop it!"

Richard froze. There was an annoyed, elevated quality to Melissa's voice that didn't sound right.

His body tense, he padded closer to the kitchen.

Melissa was definitely not all right. Barry had wrapped her up like a boa constrictor with his head buried in her neck as though he was a fucking vampire.

Melissa grunted and pushed at him, which had about as much effect as a sparrow flapping at a hawk—Spencer was a big bastard.

An image from his nightmares wavered in front of Richard's eyes—Melissa faded away, replaced by a petite woman, long blonde hair, a look of terror on her face, wrestling with a huge brute of a man, screaming out—

"Get off me, Barry. Now!"

Richard shook his head, the sound of Melissa's voice shattering the image like a shower of glass, but not before a change came over him, cold anger of the sort he hadn't felt in years, and his first reaction was to haul Barry off Melissa and pound him into the ground. Rearrange his face a few times.

Fists clenched, he gritted his teeth, fighting the urge to go off half-cocked—a bad habit of his where women were concerned. This time he had to keep a cool head. This time he'd use his brain because he wasn't going to fuck up again and have somebody else pay the price.

He quickly backtracked to the front door.

Hand on the knob, he opened the door again and then slammed it shut with enough force to rattle the windowpanes. If they didn't hear that, they were both deaf.

"Hello, darling. I'm home," he called out as he walked back through the house.

This time Spencer was sitting on the bar stool at the kitchen nook, his eyes looking Richard over with the sharp, assessing stare of a man checking to see if he could take an opponent. And after what he'd seen, if Spencer wanted to give it a shot, Richard would be more than happy to accommodate him.

Melissa was behind the counter, red spots on her cheeks showing how flushed and agitated she was. He was even more surprised when she rushed over to him and wound her arms around his neck, latching on tight as if he were a life preserver.

His arm wrapped around her waist, pulling her close. Her body was a mass of trembles.

"Miss me, puss?" he whispered in her ear.

"More than you'll know," she replied, and rested her forehead against his.

He doubted that, if what he'd seen was any indication of what she'd been putting up with before he arrived. She had a reddish mark on her neck, probably from the five o'clock shadow Barry was sporting, which just made Richard more furious.

Somehow he reined in the anger enough to give her the gentleness he sensed she needed and cradled her face in both hands to kiss her.

Melissa stiffened a little, probably because of Barry, but after a second or two her body softened against his and he forgot he was supposed to be pretending.

Pretending, nothing!

When Melissa moved into the kiss, he couldn't let go even if his life depended on it. He closed his eyes, conscious only of the feel of her soft lips sliding against his like silk, the raspy feel of her tongue slipping alongside his. Energy sparked between them, especially where her hips nestled up against his groin.

His hands slid down over her shoulders, pausing briefly over her rib cage before they settled on her hips.

"Now that's the way a man likes to be greeted," he whispered, his breath tickling her ear so that she shivered.

Keeping one arm around Melissa's waist, he lifted her left hand, ridiculously pleased to see the ring was there, and kissed it before turning to face her ex. Old Barry looked as if he were about to blow a fuse. *Good. Get the message, dickhead — she's taken.* "You must be Barry."

He held out his right hand, not through any concept of good manners, or to promote a façade of friendliness. What most women didn't understand was that shaking hands among men was often more than a courtesy — much more. It was the quickest and most opportune way to either assess an opponent or deliver an unmistakable message. Richard smiled tightly when, as anticipated, Barry tried to squeeze his bones to powder. Fine, message received. If Spencer wanted a pissing contest over Melissa, that's what he'd get.

* * * * *

Richard stood at the door, holding it open while he waited for Spencer to get his shit together and his goodbyes done with. Richard didn't care if he never saw the man again. The only reason he'd been invited to stay for dinner was because Melissa had followed Richard into the bathroom when he went to take a shower and told him she wanted Barry to really see them together—drive the message home that she had a new life, a life he wasn't part of. And hopefully him seeing them together in *their* place would seal it.

Damn right!

"I'll be in London a couple more days, Mel. I'm at the Dorchester."

Yeah, yeah, thought Richard. *Just move it on out, twat.*

Richard's blood pressure hit dangerous levels when Barry placed his hands on Melissa's shoulders and kissed her. Melissa stiffened, her eyes wide as she pushed against her ex. Richard placed a warning hand on Barry's shoulder and tightened his grip.

"Take your hands off my woman, Spencer," he uttered slowly, rage from earlier still simmering just beneath the surface, "unless you want them broken. Don't think you can abuse our hospitality, because with one phone call I can have you on a plane out of Heathrow before you can blink. I don't fucking care who you think you are."

Barry released her and laughed. He was the only one who was amused.

"No need to overreact." The smile dropped and Barry looked at Melissa, his eyes boring into hers with an intent expression that was blatantly possessive. "Later, Melissa."

The minute the door slammed shut behind him, Melissa rushed at Richard. Her body was shaking and he wrapped her up close.

"Thank you, Rich. I mean it. I couldn't have gotten through that without you."

"That's what I'm here for, puss."

"I know, but you really went above and beyond what I had any right to expect. You were brilliant. So convincing."

She lifted her head, a small smile on her face. "You nearly had *me* convinced."

"This is not a game, Melissa."

"I know. Barry doesn't give up. When he wants something, thinks something is his…"

Melissa pulled out of his arms and walked into the kitchen. As if she were chilled, she kept rubbing her hands up her arms, a noticeable shiver going over her body. The night wasn't all that cold. In fact, Richard was dressed in nothing more than a T-shirt and jeans.

Warning bells started a soft little chime in Richard's head. Was there something more about Barry that he didn't know?

"Melissa?"

She turned back to him, a big smile on her face that was about as fake as the ring she was wearing on her finger. Except the ring, at least, was a pretty good facsimile. The grin didn't cut it in any way, shape or form.

"Sorry for keeping you from all your adoring fans. It won't be for much longer."

"Don't go there, puss," he said softly.

"Well, let's face it, every woman wants you, Rich."

"Mel…" he warned. Barry had shaken her, that much was obvious, but he refused to let her take them down this path.

Her eyes started to water and she looked away quickly. "Sorry, just having a bit of trouble understanding why you're here with me when you could be with one of them."

This was garbage. And the sight of those tears was wrenching at his gut and a few other places he didn't want to think about. "What the hell did that bastard say to you before I got here, Melissa? This isn't like you. And I may have my faults, but I'm nothing like him."

"I know that."

"Do you?"

"I know you'd never treat a woman badly, Richard. You love them. *All* of them...often."

"What the— Would you stop bringing other women into this? I'm here with you. You. Not one of them. And I'm here because I want to be. Why the hell can't you see that?"

She stood there speechless, her mouth open. He realized then he'd been nearly shouting at her. But the night—and Spencer—had them both on edge.

He grabbed her hand and held it firmly against his cock so that her palm cupped every rigid, aching inch of the bulge in his jeans. "Feel this, love? This is for you. This is *because* of you. I've had this since the second you opened the door to me yesterday. And damn it, I want to be inside you." He wrapped his other hand around her neck, pulling her closer so that he could nibble at the soft skin. "I need you, Melissa. Right here, right now. Just seeing Barry's hands on you tonight..."

"When?"

"When I walked in the first time." He lifted his eyes to her. "It made me crazy."

She looked surprised, but he didn't pause to explain, to think. Grabbing her face, he slashed his lips over hers, claiming her mouth. Hard, bruising. And when her arms linked around his neck, tightening, pulling her curves more firmly against him, he felt like growling with satisfaction.

She wanted him. And he couldn't wait a moment longer.

Two stumbling steps brought them up against the kitchen counter. He placed his hands under her buttocks and hoisted her higher, tugging her skirt up to sit over her hips. He groaned into her mouth when her legs wrapped around his waist, her ankles locking against the dip in his back to align the dampness of her pussy over the thick shaft in his jeans.

Using her hold around his neck as leverage, she moaned and writhed against him until he felt as if he'd explode. When he tried to pull back, she held on tighter, nipping his lower lip until he answered in a frenzy of lust and passion, moving his mouth roughly over hers, taking everything she offered. Wanting more. Needing it all.

He reached between their bodies, frantically undoing the buttons of her blouse, tugging on the final one until it popped free, his fingers searching out the tight little nipple he could feel digging into his chest.

With a tug on the lace of her bra, he freed a rosy tip, tweaking it, and when she moaned louder, pinched it until the tip reddened and hardened, leaving a large, delicious berry for him to suck on.

Leaving her breast, he trailed his hand along the plump curves of her buttocks to the thin strap of her thong and jerked it sharply until it ripped. Moving the lacy tatters aside, he found the damp, plump lips of her pussy and stroked up the folds until he reached the sensitive nub of her clit.

As he circled it slowly, she arched in his arms, tearing her mouth free from his, panting as she tried to speak.

"Yes, God yes, Rich…"

He rested his head on her chest as she bucked against him, trying to get nearer as he pulled her closer to the edge of the counter. Then, unable to resist the tempting dew that coated his fingers, he slipped one inside the slick walls, feeling the sucking grip of her muscles as he moved in and out.

"No, stop—"

Ignoring her whispered plea, he added a second finger to the first, swirling around her clit with the broad pad of his thumb. She was so close. Christ, he could feel her inner muscles starting to clench.

"Richard," she gasped, "wait…wait…"

"For what, love?"

And then she tipped her head forward and looked at him—her green eyes, the irises dilated with pleasure, the lids heavy in her lust—and he was spellbound.

He withdrew his fingers slowly, raking them up along her clit, feeling a shudder race over her body as he did so.

"What? Tell me."

Instead of words, her shaky hand moved to his jeans, fiddling with the top stud until it popped open. Understanding dawned and he eased away a little, his hand moving between their joined bodies so he could lower the zipper. Heart pounding in his chest, he waited for her next move. A breathed a puff of relief as she freed his cramped erection.

Her hand was warm as she gripped his length. He watched, his body taut, as she directed him until he was pointing at her pussy.

They were moving so fast, but he couldn't stop, couldn't risk the moment being lost forever, and he moved closer, pausing for a heartbeat when the slick lips of her cunt opened around the weeping crest of his cock. He looked into her eyes, the question there—yes or no?—wondering if he'd be strong enough to pull back if she decided this wasn't what she wanted. Instead she pulled him to her, kissing him twice on the lips before moving to his ear.

"Now." Her breath made goose bumps race over his flesh.

He groaned at the sound of the little gasps escaping her mouth as her pulse rate rose. He felt as though he'd waited a lifetime to hear them.

"I'm sorry, love," he gasped against her neck, biting on the soft flesh and sucking until she shivered against him, "but this one will be fast and hard."

"I don't care," she moaned as the fat head slipped farther inside, eased by the rush of juices slipping down to moisten the walls of her sheath.

"Hold on to me."

Two hard thrusts through the gripping tightness of her channel and he was buried completely, his balls pulled up tight against the base of his cock.

"Yes! Damn!" His cock felt as though it were on fire.

Like liquid silk, her channel wrapped around his cock. Sensations shot through him, intense, scorching.

He bit into her neck as he withdrew slowly, raking over the slick walls of her vagina. Christ, it was so good! With an involuntary jerk, he sank inside her again.

His knees nearly buckled as he dragged out, and he released her neck to suck in a breath of air. Eyes closed with the incredible pleasure, he prepared to surge in again, his buttocks clenching for the thrust when two small hands punched at his chest. He opened his eyes and blinked, a small chuckle escaping his mouth at the look of frustration on her face.

"Don't tease!" She exhaled with relief as he slid his cock back in, the slow rake over sensitive flesh torturing them both.

The ultrasenstive skin of his cock burned with pleasure as it scraped over the slick folds. He nudged the head of her cervix and grunted.

Fully seated in her pulsing warmth, he sucked in hard breaths as his heart hammered away in his chest.

He gritted his teeth at the feel of her warmth pulling at him, drawing him in.

Her hands left his shoulders to hold his face in her palms. And then she kissed him. Holding nothing back, no barriers between them, she fucked his mouth with her tongue, setting off a chain reaction lower down so that he began to pound into her, his hands gripping tight to her ass as he shafted her roughly, a shared sense of desperation pushing at them as he battered at her cunt.

Little whimpers started to escape her mouth in time with the fluttering spasms rippling around his cock. Breaking the kiss, she tightened her hold around his neck, her legs locked tight around his waist as shudders vibrated through her body. Hearing the little mewing noises she made so close to his ear as she came, he gave up control, surrendering to the need to come that churned through him.

With a loud groan, he made a final thrust and stilled, buried so deep he felt a part of her. Lightning streaked up from his tight sac to shoot along his shaft, then the exquisite bliss of release as his cock pumped and pumped, hard, wrenching jets that made his buttocks clench and his toes curl.

It seemed as though hours passed before they both came down from the incredible high. His legs weak, he stepped backward with her wrapped around him, his cock still lodged inside her, until he felt the barstool Barry had been sitting on earlier. Flopping the short distance down, he let out a small groan as his cock, still semi-hard in spite of the force of his orgasm, was driven deep once more.

They sat there, Melissa wrapped securely around him, their bodies sweaty and sticky, for who knew how long, until their breaths slowed and their hearts stopped pounding.

He reached up a hand and smoothed the hair off her face, noticing the swollen lips, the telltale flush on her skin.

"You okay, love?"

"I'm fine, Rich. Dead, I think, but fine." A weak chuckle accompanied her words.

"Any time, any place, eh, Melissa?"

Richard's head shot up at the voice and twisted around to glance over Melissa's shoulder at Barry leaning against the doorjamb into the kitchen. That cold fist of anger coiled in Richard's chest again as Melissa gasped against his neck, holding on to him so tightly it was as though she were trying to climb inside.

"How long have you been standing there?" Richard gritted out.

You smarmy prick, Richard thought. Melissa was embarrassed as hell, couldn't Barry see that? The only thing saving her ex from a fist in his face was the fact it would leave Melissa exposed, and she was his main concern right now. He turned them around, shielding Melissa's body with his own as he stood. Then he helped her pull down her skirt and straighten her blouse. "You ever heard of knocking?" he asked when he faced Barry, his arm around Melissa keeping her behind his back.

"Oh, I knocked. Twice. No one answered. And since the door was still unlocked…"

"Why are you here, Spencer? I thought you'd gone."

"Forgot my room key for the hotel. I certainly didn't expect to see Melissa acting like a tramp. Again."

Richard's body tensed, and he would have taken a swing at Barry, but Melissa's hand on his arm stalled him. His body stayed coiled though, ready to lash out.

Who the fuck did this prick think he was? The morality police? Richard's fists clenched and unclenched in frustrated impotence as a more detailed picture of Melissa's life with Spencer, outside of what Tom and Melissa had already let slip, began to form. And it was a picture Richard didn't like one little bit.

Showing Barry his back, he turned and walked Melissa to the bedroom. Once there, out of Barry's sight, he cradled Melissa's face and eased her closer.

"Sorry about that, love. You okay?"

"Yeah, it was just a shock. It was such a…a private moment…special, you know?"

Richard knew exactly what she meant. His mind was still reeling.

"And he made me feel dirty. I'm not a tramp, Richard."

"I know that, love."

"How dare he! I'd like to go out there and give him a swift kick in the balls."

"Right behind me, puss. I'll go get rid of him. Why don't you freshen up, get ready for bed."

She nodded and headed into the bathroom. When he heard the shower running, he pulled the door closed behind him, returning to face Melissa's ex, a man he was growing to actively dislike more and more by the second.

Spencer still had that disapproving cast to his face. "I was training her to be a lady. A woman who could hold her place in society. And *you*...you of all people should know better. You're turning her into a slut. In a kitchen, no less!"

Richard took a deep breath and reined in the hands that were just itching to beat the snot out of Melissa's ex.

"You fucking hypocrite," he said, his voice a low growl. "You were pawing all over her when I first walked in tonight. If it weren't for the fact that Melissa has been upset enough for one night, I'd knock your bloody block off. Besides, what you interrupted was a private moment between me and the woman who is going to be *my* wife. Mine, not yours. So I suggest you leave, Spencer. And not just this house—the UK. Go back home. You're neither wanted nor needed."

Barry's expression hardened. "You cut to the chase. I like that. No messing around with you Brits. But see, Melissa *will* be coming home with me. She's mine, *Rich*. We Spencers don't give up what's ours—ever."

Richard stiffened, hearing those words for what they were—a gantlet thrown in his face. "You just don't get it, do you? Melissa has obviously moved on from you. It's over. So stay away from her. I mean it. Or you won't just answer to me. Believe me, you don't want to bring the kind of trouble down on yourself that I can muster."

"Are you threatening me?" Spencer asked incredulously.

"Let's just call it a warning..." Richard had been so focused on Barry, he hadn't noticed the door open, or Alex's silent entry. But at the sound of Alex's deep voice, Richard let some of the tension bleed from his taut muscles.

Spencer spun around, his mouth dropping open a little when he caught sight of Alex looming behind him. Alex had that effect on people. At six foot two, Richard wasn't exactly short, and for that matter, Barry and he were a pretty even match, but Alex towered at least a full head over both of them. For a large man, though, he moved with a deadly stealth.

"Melissa told us all about you, Mr. Spencer. Now she and Richard have paid you the courtesy of allowing you to see her and confirm that she's happy, but from where Richard and I are standing, you've overstayed your welcome."

Spencer's eyes shot from Alex to Richard and back again. He looked confused, uncomprehending at the introduction of another possible player into the game. Richard could almost see his mind ticking over, trying to work out this added dynamic. "And who you might you be?"

"Alex?" Melissa, wrapped up now in a woolen sweater and a pair of black stretch pants, her face washed clean of makeup and her hair damp from her shower, came rushing into the kitchen, the confusion on her face clearing as a wide smile lit up her face. "Alex!" She ran the last few steps and rushed at him, a little giggle erupting as he lifted her easily and kissed her.

Richard watched in heated fascination as Alex took his time—as he did with everything. Watching the two of them, rather than making him angry as it did earlier with Spencer, made him burn with hunger for more of what he knew Alex and he could give Melissa. Alex's timing, as usual, was impeccable. And the inference Melissa was unwittingly giving about the three of them...well, if nothing else made Spencer give up his lost cause, that should. When her legs wrapped around Alex's hips and a small whimper of pleasure left her mouth, Richard smiled and glanced at Spencer.

"In case your high moral ground prevents you from grasping the significance, *old chap*, what we three have is a *ménage a trois*. Melissa is engaged to both of us, and Alex and I don't give up what's ours—*ever*."

"You fucking perverts! You're corrupting her," gasped Spencer. Judging from the redness of his face and the glare in his eyes, Barry needed a blood pressure check soon before he sparked a massive stroke. Then he changed, his livid expression evening out in the blink of an eye. It happened so fast, Richard blinked to make sure he hadn't imagined it.

When Alex finally pulled back from the kiss, Melissa kept her arms wrapped tightly around his neck.

"Good to have me home, baby?" murmured Alex against her ear.

"I've missed you."

As "homecomings" went, even Richard was impressed. The two of them looked like the real thing.

Richard walked over to place his hands on Melissa's waist from behind and he and Alex both turned to look at Spencer, the message they were sending him explicit. "It's time you left," said Richard. "I'd say Melissa has made her decision, wouldn't you?"

"It's not too late, Mel honey. You don't have to do this," said Barry, a hint of desperation in his tone.

Alex remained calm, as always, his voice not even rising as he said, "No one is forcing Melissa to do anything, Spencer—ever. She wants this—we all do. You blew it and now she's ours."

With an abrupt "We'll see," Barry Spencer turned and walked out.

Richard followed and after the door slammed shut, locked it with a feeling of satisfaction. All up, things had turned out pretty well.

"I'll hand it to you, Melissa—with you, things are never dull."

There was no response and Richard walked back into the kitchen to find Melissa and Alex looking intently at each other before Alex began to slowly kiss her, moving his mouth over hers before really settling into the kiss. He caught a glimpse of

Alex's tongue disappearing into Melissa's mouth before he began to plunder, and fiery arousal scorched through Richard, threatening to overwhelm him.

His need to be a part of them, sharing the touches, the passion, punched him in the gut and left his cock hard and throbbing. Fuck, he was on shaky ground and he knew it. He and Alex had shared women, he'd watched his friend making the moves, and the hunger had always been there to make it complete.

But never like this.

But would Melissa agree?

She had to. The look on Alex's face as he pulled back said it all. Melissa was more than "special" to him—he suspected Alex had never gotten Melissa out of his system.

He couldn't stay away and moved in behind her, positioning his chest against her back, hands on her waist again. He lifted a hand to move her long hair out of the way until he could taste the skin of her neck, her shoulder. "You've done it now, puss. You realize that, don't you? Your reputation is damaged beyond repair."

"This is kinda kinky, isn't it?" she whispered, her eyes ranging over Alex's face.

In spite of the sexual tension coiling in his body, forcing him to rub his cock up against her buttocks, Richard forced a chuckle. "At least that's better than 'weird'."

Melissa's mouth lifted in a small smile in response to Alex's. "You two know each other. Why am I not surprised?"

"Melissa Blake," said Richard, nipping at her ear lobe, his hands moving beneath her sweater to settle just under the temptation of her gorgeous tits, "meet my best friend, my comrade in arms for more years than either of us care to recall, Alex Ryan."

As his mouth moved to her shoulder, nibbling on the small square of exposed flesh, she gasped.

"You ever been with two men, baby?" Alex asked, his voice low, a little bit rough.

Her body arched into Alex's as Richard's hands settled over her breasts, pinching the nipples. "N-No. Never."

"Interested?"

"I've never thought about it."

"Start thinking then," said Alex, before he winked at Richard and covered Melissa's mouth with his, swallowing the moan as Richard bit down on the side of her neck and sucked.

Chapter Four

Melissa shivered, nervous at the surprising development. She hadn't expected to suddenly find herself trapped between the two of them. It was like being wrapped up in a big testosterone blanket. Safe. Warm. And incredibly sexy.

She couldn't blame them—what else were they to think when she pretty much jumped on Alex the moment she saw him? After the evening she'd had, she'd just been so glad to see him again. No matter what, he always made her feel special, as though he really cared. And he did—she had no doubts on that score.

Richard's reaction had amazed her though. Even if they were pretending for Barry's sake, she and Richard had shared some pretty intense moments over the past twenty-four hours, enough, certainly, for most guys to be feeling a touch of ownership about the affair. So what man wanted "his woman" wrapping her body and her mouth around another man?

Apparently these two, judging from the way they were mashing up against her as though she were a Melissa sandwich.

In spite of her nerves, she couldn't deny her body's response to the situation. The moment Richard had moved behind her, the heat of his torso rubbing against hers, warming her, her legs had weakened, her body turning fluid, unexpectedly needy. And between her legs, she could feel her labia swelling, slickening, as the thought of what they could do to her raced through her mind.

She was shocked to discover she wasn't at all uncomfortable in what was a blatantly kinky sexual position. In fact...if she just spread her legs a little more and Alex pushed a little harder... She licked her lips as she looked up at him.

"Don't look at me like that, baby," Alex growled.

Look at him like what? When he used that low, sexy voice, her whole body turned to mush. Besides, the way Alex was looking at her, the look that always said he wanted to strip her naked and have his way with her, was giving her goose bumps all over. And there was something about Alex saying "baby" in his deep voice that set off her hormones and made her knees go weak.

She took a deep breath, trying to regain some control of her fluttery pulse, but he was so close, all she could inhale was him, that indefinable masculine scent that made her want to bury her face in his chest and just breathe him in. God, he smelled and tasted so good. Not that Richard behind her was any less gorgeous. But as it had been with Richard, from the first moment she and Alex had locked eyes all those months ago, it had been an instant connection. Hot. Sizzling. And when he kissed her...

A whimper escaped as Alex's finger freed the front catch on her bra. Then Richard's hands were raising her sweater, his warm hands easing the cups of her bra aside to palm her breasts in his big hands.

Alex stepped back a little, leaving her feeling exposed, vulnerable.

"Christ, you're beautiful." His expression darkened, became voracious as Richard lifted her breasts to Alex, offering them.

Oh God. She sucked in a gasp as Alex's lips closed around a nipple and began to suck. The drawing, pulling sensation sent liquid heat coursing through her body, to pool lower down and spike her clit. A sharp pinch on the other nipple had her arching toward him.

"Easy, love," came Richard's voice in her ear. "You're beautiful. Let us do this."

She moaned, unsure what she wanted, but knowing she needed something more.

Richard's hold on her tightened and he ground his erection against her, rubbing up and down the crease of her buttocks. "Shhh, puss, it's okay. We'll take care of you.

There was something wicked and naughty about standing between the two of them like this, but she was beyond caring. All she knew was that she needed. Now.

When Alex began to rub his groin against her, her legs nearly gave way. A sharp bite on her nipple made her moan. But when Richard's hand skated down between her and Alex's bodies, under the waistband of her pants to cup her mound, she let out a cry. His finger circled her engorged clit before sliding between the slick lips of her pussy to thrust into her channel. The steady rhythm was making her crazy. She needed more to push her over the peak she could feel building.

When Alex moved to her other breast, licking around the sensitive peak before closing his mouth around the nipple to suck hard, her body bucked against him, tremors building as she crumbled under the sensual assault.

Her fingers gripped Alex's head, holding him tight against her. Her body was readying, her tummy tightening, the walls of her cunt clenching as the orgasm began to power through her.

She barely had time to suck in a ragged breath before Alex lifted his head to kiss her again, his mouth moving over hers—hard, possessive, his tongue thrusting in and out—and she surrendered to the decadent sensations, a cry escaping as Richard bit her neck, and she shattered.

The two men continued to pet and gentle her as her wits slowly returned. Soothing her with quiet words and soft touches.

She sagged in Richard's hold as Alex stepped away, the heated look he gave her going straight to her clit.

"Fuck, I have to go, baby," gritted out Alex. "But for now Richard will take care of you, okay?" His smile, the way he stroked her face and the look in his eyes, was so tender, so loving, all she could do was nod, unable to speak over the lump in her throat. Her eyes started to water. What was wrong with her emotions?

Richard turned her then and his expression was so pleased, so…content, she just wanted to bask in its glow.

He kissed her slowly, twining his tongue with hers in a leisurely tangle, taking his time until the only breath she could take was his.

When he broke away, her head was spinning.

"Richard, I need a word before I go."

Richard grinned and brushed a quick kiss over her lips. "Back in a minute, puss." With his arm around her waist, he walked her toward the bedroom. "Why don't you jump into bed and I'll join you in a minute?"

She stood there and nodded dumbly. The power of speech seemed to have deserted her.

Before Alex reached the door, he turned with his hand on the knob. "Be careful, baby. If you need either of us, you call and we'll be there."

He seemed to be waiting on an answer so she nodded again, forcing words out of her mouth, "S-Sure. I will."

She watched them both walk out the door and reached for the wall with a shaky hand.

What a night. She shook her head and exhaled. Too many things had happened too quickly, and suddenly, without either Richard or Alex there, tiredness overcame her.

In the bedroom, she stripped out of her clothes then climbed into bed. Her mind seemed unable to think of anything but the little scene in the kitchen. As her eyes closed she imagined what it would be like to be between the two of them in her bed…

Velvet Ties

* * * * *

Richard leaned up against Alex's Mercedes and crossed his arms over his chest, waiting for Alex to speak. He felt wired, over the top from what had happened. All he wanted was for Alex and him to return to Melissa, take her to bed and pleasure her until she begged them to stop.

"You okay?" asked Alex.

"Yeah, fine," he said, pushing away the biting edge of hunger that was shredding at his control. It hadn't been this raw with Cilla even in the early days. All he could think about was getting back to Melissa, plunging inside her while Alex held her, and listening to her cry out both their names as she clenched around his cock.

"You don't look fine—"

"Don't worry about me—I'll handle it. What's up?" Richard said, changing the direction of Alex's thoughts.

"I made some calls as soon as you left my office tonight. Intel's started coming in."

"That was fast."

Alex grinned. "I only employ the best."

"And?"

Alex stood with his hands in his slacks, the pose relaxed but Richard knew he was still wired from the scene with Melissa. Christ, any man with half a dick would be.

"Spencer's had two investigators looking for Melissa since she skipped out on him."

"Sounds determined."

"Obsessed is what I'm hearing. That's not good, Richard. He has the money, resources, the motivation and to his mind, the reason, to get what he wants. Don't underestimate him."

"Point taken."

"And I didn't want Melissa to know—she'd probably freak out—but you need to know. I've got one of my men watching her during the day. Just in case. Something about Spencer..." Alex's eyes narrowed as he glanced over at Melissa's little two-bedroom maisonette. "That old gut feeling, you know?"

"I hear what you're saying. Felt it too."

"Anyway, I've given Derek your number so if something goes down, he can reach either of us." Then Alex looked at him with a slow smile creasing his face. "I better get going. Let you get to bed."

"Jealous?"

"As hell."

"You could join us."

"Bastard! Tempting—fuck," Alex groaned, "you have no idea. But not tonight. Melissa's too shaken up."

"She responded, Alex. She wants it. Wants what we can give her. That response was no mistake."

"Maybe. We'll see." Alex stared at Melissa's front door as if considering changing his mind then reached for his car door and opened it, resting his foot on the runner, his arms on the roof. "I'm fucking horny as hell. Get back in there, you dumb bastard. Or I'll switch places with you in a heartbeat."

Richard laughed. "I'm going. I'm going."

He shut the front door as he heard the Mercedes pull away and purr down the street.

Bloody hell, what a night!

Melissa was nowhere around. He turned off the lights and headed into the bedroom to find her curled up under the quilt, sound asleep. He was horny too, but after what she'd been through, he figured she needed her sleep.

Five minutes later he was curled up behind her and shut his eyes. But images of Melissa between Alex and him, what it would feel and look like to watch her writhe in pleasure as she came apart in their arms, played out behind his closed lids. With a muffled groan, he grabbed hold of his erection, clenching it tightly in his fist before he was tempted to put it somewhere else, somewhere infinitely more pleasurable. But in the back of his mind was the realization that what the three of them shared was a rare connection and it had moved swiftly beyond the point of just "damn good sex". Erotic images filled his mind of Melissa crying out between them, begging for more.

His cock began to leak and he wiped the pearl of moisture over the crown, jerking as he abraded the band of nerves running up the back of the crest with his rough hands.

They'd take her—rough, hard, slow, soft—and she'd burn for them.

* * * * *

"Well, look what the cat dragged in…"

Richard tried to hide the grin as he closed the front door to Melissa's office behind him. "Good to see you too, Cynthia."

"I wondered when we'd see you around here again."

"Miss me?"

"Like a boil on my butt."

He laughed. He couldn't help it. Today he was just feeling too good to let the jibes from Melissa's disapproving secretary needle him. She reminded him of his Aunt Joy even down to the graying hair pulled back into a neat bun and the immaculate skirt suits she always wore. Not a hair out of place. Nothing flustered her—least of all him. All vim and vinegar on the outside, but a marshmallow center—especially where Melissa was concerned. With no kids of her own, he'd always had the impression Cynthia had unofficially adopted Melissa. She fussed over her like a mother hen. And after his and Melissa's breakup, she sure didn't like him. That point had been made abundantly clear when he'd called on Melissa not long after, trying to patch things up.

"Melissa told me to send you through if you dropped by." He could tell by the look on her face she disapproved of that idea too. "You the reason for that crass display of wealth on her finger?"

"Crass? I have very good taste, thank you very much."

"That remains to be seen, but if you've finally gotten your head on straight and decided to marry Melissa, I guess that could be true. Although personally I think she could have done much better."

"And I love you too." Amazing. Not even Cynthia's pointed digs could rattle his mood. "So, can I see my lovely fiancée? I'd like to take her to lunch."

"Well, it certainly is her day for lunch invitations. In fact, I'd say you had some competition, except that she looked less happy to see the other gentleman than I am to see you."

Richard's smile—and good mood—dropped. Suspicion raised its head in his mind. "Describe him to me."

"I told you she wasn't happy—"

"Humor me, Cynthia. She's been having trouble with an unwanted admirer lately. Was he Australian?"

Cynthia frowned. "Yes, I believe he was."

"And he left?"

"Reluctantly, but yes. Pushy fellow. Melissa waited about ten minutes, then went out herself. Now that you mention it, she was quite discombobulated."

"That sounds like him." Richard walked toward the door. "Where did she go?"

"Alfredo's. Around the corner. On Wednesdays, Alfredo makes cannelloni. It's her favorite."

"Look, I know you don't like me, Cynthia, but do me a favor—if he drops in again, call me."

He raced out the door. He just hoped Derek was on the job. That sneaky bastard Spencer. Going behind his back.

He jogged the short distance to the restaurant. A quick glance around didn't reveal Derek, so either he was inside or well concealed. Fortunately the lunch crowd was thin and he spotted Melissa immediately at a table near the latticed windows at the back. His mood went south in a big way when he saw Spencer's big paw swamp Melissa's smaller hand and her withdraw it quickly, her eyes flaring with anger.

A shake of his head and a nod in their direction let the hostess know he knew where he was going. As he approached the table, he took a deep breath, noticing then a large man watching him closely but discreetly from a table nearby. A small wink that could have passed as a facial tic, and he guessed that was Derek letting him know he was on the job. A small measure of relief took the edge off, replacing the disquiet that had filled him in Melissa's office.

When he stood in front of their table, Melissa looked up, surprise replacing the anger on her face. "Richard?"

"Hello, darling." He leaned over to kiss her, wanting to rub Spencer's nose in the display of affection. "Hope you don't mind me not calling first, but a client cancelled and I thought I'd take you to lunch."

"No, I don't mind at all." She eyes narrowed as she looked worriedly at Richard.

Richard pulled a vacant chair over from a nearby table and sat next to Melissa, close enough to place his arm around her, and looked over at Barry. "Let me guess, Spencer, you were conveniently in the vicinity and thought you'd drop in..."

A hard glint flickered into Spencer's eyes. There and gone. "Actually, I can't stay. I have another appointment to attend shortly. I'll be in touch, Mel. There are things we need to tie up before I head back to Sydney. Perhaps we could have lunch tomorrow?"

"I don't think so, Barry. There's nothing to discuss."

Barry shrugged. "I'll call. You may change your mind when you hear what I have to say, sweetness." He nodded his head at Richard. "Danville." Then stood and left.

Derek rose, shook his head at the approaching waitress and left too.

Sweetness, Richard snorted. The use of the endearment teed him off, but all up, the confrontation was almost an anticlimax. He had been ready to use physical force if necessary, and had to shake off the kick from the flood of adrenaline. He turned to see Melissa looking at him curiously.

"You thought you'd take me to lunch?"

He forced a smile. "Yes. You hungry? I'm starved."

"Bullshit." Melissa placed her clasped hands on her folded menu and looked at him. Waiting.

"Actually, I am starving." He leaned over to murmur in her ear, "Somebody made me miss breakfast this morning," Satisfaction filled him as a dimple peeked out. He may have missed breakfast, but it was worth it for the little interlude that had taken place in Melissa's shower. Maybe she should look into getting a larger hot water heater…or maybe they should move to his or Alex's place. They were going to need lots of space after all…

"You are a sex maniac," she whispered.

"You loved it." His hand ducked under the table, caressing her knee and beginning a slow slide up her leg. Silky stockings. Thigh highs. That much he knew. Even after coming so hard his legs nearly buckled in the shower, just watching Melissa dressing for work was all it had taken to rev him up again, and he'd been panting like a horny dog by the time he'd watched her pull those sexy stockings up her legs. His fingers reached the elasticized lace at the top and traced the line of it down between her legs.

"Richard!" she whispered. "We're in public."

"No one can see." He'd made sure of that, placing his body between her and the four tables of other diners. Lucky the lunch crowd was light. The thing was though, he couldn't help himself. This close to her and he had to touch.

"So, you want to tell me about this little meeting between you and Barry?"

"What are you implying? That I asked to him to meet me?" The green in her eyes deepened as she became incensed and she pushed his hand aside, eventually dragging it up to place it on the table. "It wasn't a *meeting*. I didn't ask to see him—in fact I told him no when he came to my office. But *he* followed *me* here. And rather than make a scene and disrupt the other patrons, I thought if I approached it calmly, I could make him see that I had every intention of committing to you and Alex." She paused, a little crease forming on her forehead. "Boy, that sounds weird. Besides, I thought here, in a public place, I'd be fine."

"Why didn't you call me?"

"Why would I?"

"Because I'm your fiancé."

Her expression was incredulous. "Exactly. I asked for a fiancé, not a bodyguard. That would be asking a bit much of any man. Besides, I think Barry's getting the idea. He's not stupid. And after that little added scene with Alex last night..."

Richard smiled inside at the way her hand moved nervously up to her neck. He'd noticed a nice little bite mark there this morning, to match the one Alex had apparently placed on the upper slope of her breast. That caveman feeling was coming back and he had to stifle the smile it brought. He rubbed a finger over where he knew the mark on her neck was hidden by the blouse. "Sore? I could kiss it better, puss," he suggested with a waggle of his eyebrows. "Or the other one..." His finger traced a line down the soft cotton of her blouse over the swell of her left breast. Melissa's face was flushed, her breaths coming faster when he raised his eyes back to hers.

"No, it's fine, thanks. Anyway, I'm quite sure Barry wouldn't want to touch me with a ten-foot barge pole now."

Richard begged to differ, especially after seeing the proprietary way Barry was looking at her when he arrived. "So what did he want?"

"I don't know. We'd only been here a few minutes before you arrived. Then he left."

"I don't want you alone with him, Melissa." With a finger, he turned her face fully toward him and brushed a soft kiss over her lips. "Promise me."

"You're taking your role in this awfully seriously."

Her eyes searched his and he looked away. Melissa had an uncanny way of seeing right through him when she had a mind. "You're right—you're my fiancée, so your protection is my responsibility."

He risked a glance at her to see her eyes narrowing at him. "Is there something you're not telling me, Rich?"

"Such as?"

"I don't know. That's just it. You're acting…strangely, even for you."

"Me? Strange?" He looked around for the waiter. He could really do with a drink.

"Yeah. For starters, you're totally into this whole 'fiancé' thing. If she didn't know better, a girl could get ideas."

He caught the waiter's eye and mouthed *beer* and held up one finger. "Just so long as we convince Barry. Soon as he's gone…" Where was that damn waiter and his beer?

"Oh, for chrissakes, Richard, chill out. Look at you. I mention 'serious' and you're suddenly nervous as hell. You don't have to worry—I've already had my reality check with you, remember? I'm not likely to forget that in a hurry."

"That wasn't what I meant."

Melissa grabbed her handbag off the floor, pulled out her sunglasses and snapped it shut. "Who cares? And really, you know, I've kinda lost my appetite." She stood to leave.

"Hang on." He stood and grabbed her, his hand shackling her forearm.

She glared down at it then back up at him. "What now?"

"Don't leave the office tonight until I get there."

"Richard! For fuck's sake." She shrugged off his hand. "You've done your job. Barry knows—or at least he thinks—I'm taken. Ease up. Drop the act. Who's here to see? Me? Well hell, what a waste. I already know where I stand with you."

"I strongly doubt that," he muttered.

"Whatever."

"I mean it, Melissa, you leave that office before I get there tonight and I'll spank your arse so hard you won't be able to sit down for a week."

"Fine!"

"Good."

She stormed out and he followed her after dropping some money on the table to cover the beer that hadn't arrived.

When he caught up to her, grabbing her hand for appearance's sake, she just turned her head and glared at him, gritting out under her breath, "Just for the record, I feel sorry for the girl who gets lumbered with you for real, Richard Danville. I'm just glad it's not me."

* * * * *

Not caring of the potential damage he might cause, Richard slammed his mobile phone shut. *Shit.* What a night for one of his biggest corporate clients to reschedule the training sessions for three of their executives to *after* six thirty. Exactly when he told Melissa he'd be at her office to pick her up.

And if he didn't arrive on time, she wouldn't wait too long. Not with the mood she'd been in when he left her there after lunch.

The phone rang again. Alex's number showed up on the display.

He flipped it open. "Tell me you've got some good news."

"Bad day?"

"Fucking mess," Richard said, and sighed.

"Melissa?"

"Currently the number one bane of my existence. Damn woman's itching for my hand all over her arse. Right after I gag her."

"Awww, true love—ain't it sweet."

"Shove it, you sarcastic bastard. Look, I need a favor. Melissa's expecting me to pick her up at work at six thirty. But work's come up and I'm not going to make it back to her place until probably after nine. Could you meet her and take her home?"

"Derek told me about Spencer showing up. Did something else happen?"

"Not that I know of—not that she'd tell me with the mood she's in. But right now I'm not Melissa's favorite person, so if I asked her, she'd most likely tell me to take a flying leap…preferably over a field full of cow dung. I doubt I would have known he'd called in to see her if I hadn't dropped in unexpectedly to take her to lunch. There's something about him, Alex. I have this feeling something is going down."

"That's why I called. Barry Spencer has a room at the Dorchester, all right, but Derek followed him this afternoon when he left the restaurant. Spencer also has a second room. At the Crestfield."

"The what?"

"Little hotel. Two star. Not far from Melissa's."

"Why would he need two rooms?"

"Don't know, but he also had a meeting with a dealer a couple of hours after he left you and Melissa."

"A dealer? What—"

"Drugs, Richard. Get this—he purchased some roofies."

Richard went cold all over. His suspicions were becoming confirmed in the worst way. "What would Spencer want with a date-rape drug? Is he planning on raping Melissa? Someone else? What the bloody hell is going on?"

"Don't know. Don't know how that links in with the CNI we found after we swept his room at the Dorchester either."

"CNI? Do I want to know?" asked Richard.

"A Certificate of No Impediment. If a person wants to marry overseas, they need it for the wedding to be legal and binding back in their country."

The pieces were starting to fall into an odd sort of fit, and fury filled Richard. "Christ, he just never gives up, does he?"

"The main thing is, I think one of us needs to be with Melissa 24/7. I'll pick her up and take her home. You get there as soon as you can."

"Anything else?"

"Yes. I have some contacts making enquiries in Sydney, and obviously the Spencer boys are being pretty tight-lipped. The wives too. Except for one. Seems this little lady and Melissa go back a few years, pre-Barry. University, from what I'm told. She let slip that Barry's been a bit of a crazy man since Melissa left him. To say she's worried for Melissa is putting it mildly. That means we should be too." He paused. "Shit, look at the time—I better leave now if I'm going to meet Melissa at six thirty. See you later, mate."

"Thanks, Alex."

"Hey, it's no hardship for me. Just get there when you can. I'll hold the fort."

Richard shut his phone, turning pensive over Alex's news.

At least his gut feeling about Spencer was right. Small comfort when Melissa was in danger. It was the helplessness that ate at him. It was a feeling he knew all too well. Frustration at not knowing when or where the attack might come from poured through him. In his mind, the evening faded away along with the traffic and the noises of a peak-hour city. Instead, he was transported back seven years in time to a dark, rainy night. His pulse sped up, his body tensed. Sweat broke out on his brow. He couldn't let it happen again. Couldn't...

*****

Melissa sat back and considered the menu—for the second time that day. Perhaps this time she'd actually get to eat something. Just as well the afternoon had been busy as hell. This was the first time she'd had to calculate the fact that it had been almost twenty-four hours since she'd last eaten. Lunch had been a bust. Breakfast too. But then a wet, soapy Richard with wicked, sexy thoughts on his mind was pretty hard to pass up in place of a slice of toast. Pity he could be such a pain in the butt whenever he was clothed. Now if there was a way to keep him naked with sex on his mind...

No, that had been a big part of his problem last time—not with her. With the faithful Richard minions. Maybe he was just a sex addict. Was that the thing with Alex and him? Did they share all their women? No, they mustn't. She'd been with both of them and they sure as hell hadn't shared her.

A hand covering hers distracted her from her thoughts. "I beg your pardon? Did you say something?" She looked up from her menu to see Alex watching her intently. With a mental shrug, she tossed off thoughts of pissy Richard. She'd wasted enough of her afternoon trying to work him out. That was a lost cause if ever there was one.

Now Alex... Steady as a rock, what people saw was what they got. No wondering where you stood. Not to mention the man could do things to her that melted her brain and every erogenous zone in creation.

"I didn't say a thing, baby. But I think you should. What's bothering you? You've been distracted since the moment I picked you up."

"Just how close are you and Richard, Alex?"

"Very. We served together for a lot of years. Why, he bugging you?"

"Bugging me? The man is hormonal, I swear it. One minute he's giving off vibes as though he...well, as though he really *likes* me, you know? All possessive and loving. Then he pulls back and does that 'I really don't give a shit' number. 'This is just pretend.' Talk about unsettling."

"Don't be too hard on him, Melissa. Richard has...issues."

She could feel a lump brewing in her throat. Her eyes getting misty. *No, dammit. Not now. Not here.* "That's bullshit, Alex."

"You care, baby. Admit it."

She raised her face to his. Taking in the look of concern. But for her...or Richard? "Why should I? He's a pain in the butt. Christ, I don't know why I let him do this to me. You'd think I would have learned my lesson last time."

"What actually happened? You two together long?"

A bit of laminate off the menu was lifting and she worried it with her nail. "About six weeks. And it was lovely, for the most part." She looked at Alex. "Rich can be a very nice guy when he isn't distracted."

"Distracted?"

"He hasn't told you, I gather."

"No."

She thought back to that night. It wasn't hard—she'd replayed it in her head a million times since then, wondering if she could have—should have—done anything differently.

"We'd been out for dinner. Very romantic. Couple of bottles of very fine wine. I mean, Richard really knows how to turn it on for a girl. Makes her feel special." Melissa took a sip of the Chardonnay Alex had ordered when they sat down. "We were both a little tipsy, so we went back to his place since it was closer to the restaurant. Big mistake. Or big reality check. We'd hardly walked in the door when the first phone call came. I mean, it's a bit disconcerting when you're standing there with your man's hand…well, never mind…I'm sure you can fill in the details. And the bloody phone rings. Some bimbo called 'Precious' of all things. Precious! Christ. Anyway, Richard tells me to ignore it and we get back to…you know. By this time we actually managed to get undressed." She glared at the little smile on Alex's face. "You find this amusing?"

"Sorry, baby." He picked up her hand, kissing it, and little butterflies skipped through her tummy. "Just picturing it. Still can't figure out how Richard could keep his mind on the phone with you standing there in front of him with no clothes on."

"Yeah, well, that makes two of us. I mean, I was *naked*. Anyway, when the next one phoned, the machine took it. What is with these women, Alex? Don't they have lives? Men of their own? This one wanted him to call her 'desperately, dahling. I *need* to see you.' Give me a break. What is he running apart from that personal trainer thing — an escort service?"

"He's popular. Always has been."

"Too bloody popular for my liking."

And that was the problem in getting involved with Richard Danville. Earl of Whatever and Lord of the Sexually Needy.

"Hey."

She looked up at Alex's gentle tug on her hand. "Sorry."

"And? I get a feeling the best…or the worst is yet to come."

"Definitely worst." The mortification she'd felt that night came back to her. She took a deep breath and let it out slowly. "You ever called out the wrong woman's name in bed, Alex?"

"No." His eyebrows rose. "God, he didn't."

"Sure he did. A few minutes after Leticia left her husky little present on the answering machine." The cow. If Melissa ever met her, she'd probably sock her one right between the eyes. "So there you have it—the short and not-so sweet story of Richard and Melissa. Mind if we change the topic?" She took a too-large gulp of wine, feeling it burn a little as it went down.

"Ah, baby. It was a slip. Don't be too hard on him."

"A slip, maybe, but it doesn't change the fact that he was thinking of Leticia when he was fucking me. That doesn't gain me going soft on any man. He's with me, totally, or I'm out of there."

"And yet you let him back in again."

"Yeah, well, I was desperate. Besides," she slammed the menu shut, "this is just pretend, right?"

"He really does like you, Melissa. But there's a lot about Richard you don't know. A lot more to Richard than he lets most people see."

"So tell me. Help me understand."

"Can't, baby. That's Richard's story to tell when he's ready."

"You guys all stick together."

"For now, though, we're sticking to you. Now let's eat. Can't have you wasting away to a shadow."

"As if that's likely," she scoffed.

Later as they were walking to his car, Melissa said, "Cynthia likes you."

"She does?"

"Yeah, she thinks Richard's a dickhead."

Alex laughed. "She must be the only woman on the planet Richard hasn't charmed. Maybe he needs an image consultant. I'll have to tell him."

"Never mind Richard, what about you, Alex? How are things with you? I've missed you."

He knew Melissa was still confused over Richard and he should probably back off, but tonight he couldn't. The number of times over the past few months he'd reached for the phone to call her. God, if she knew. He wrapped an arm around her shoulder, pulling her up close as they walked. "I've missed you too, baby. A lot."

They reached his car and he pressed the button to unlock the doors.

"Really?"

Before she could open the passenger door, he backed her against it, needing to taste her again. Feel her open up under him. Sink into that magic mouth.

"More than I can put into words." *More than you'll ever know.*

She looked up at him and smiled, eyes that dark emerald green he loved, lips soft. It was a look he saw often at night when he closed his eyes. Pictured them together as they'd been. She had always been like a drug to him—breaking away from her was one of the hardest things he'd done. But they'd both needed time to heal, find their feet again. If they'd met six months later though…

How could she have no idea what she did to him…and Richard for that matter. That surprising and unexpected little interlude in her kitchen had been like throwing gasoline onto a naked flame. All night and all day he'd been sporting a giant hard-on thinking about it. About her. About the three of them.

Watching her tonight in the restaurant, he'd been amazed once more how a woman who oozed such a natural sensuality could be so oblivious to her effect on those around her. Especially men. More than once he'd noticed the interested, speculative looks men cast her way. As a man, he knew what those looks meant—they'd already pictured her naked and their cocks were busting to fuck her. He'd nipped their interest in the bud with a look that said "hands off". With that though, came a raging feeling of possessiveness that was new to him. But if anyone's cock was getting inside Melissa, it was his or

Richard's. Knowing Richard was already making love to her, waking up with her, coming inside her...

His pulse sped up, his legendary control beginning to fray. He might hide it well, but around Melissa, at times he felt like a rabid dog about to gnaw off its own foot just to get some relief. This was definitely one of them.

Melissa was beautiful, sexy as hell and driving him insane with need.

The decision was made quickly—if Richard fucked up with Melissa again, Alex was taking her anyway. He'd wasted enough time. Turning away from her this time was not an option.

"So don't tell me—show me how much you've missed me," she said.

Melissa looked up at him as the words hung in the air between them. Heads and bodies close, barely a breath separated them. Running his eyes over her face, he took in the delicate lips, slightly parted to show a hint of even, white teeth. As he watched, the tip of a pink tongue peeked out to moisten her lower lip before disappearing again.

More than anything he wanted to follow that tongue. Sink into the warm recesses and taste and taste until she couldn't refuse him anything. As he lowered his head, he watched her eyes flutter closed, lips parting on a breath, ready... A light brush, the softest of touches, he moved his mouth over hers, relishing the feel of her lips softening under his before his hunger got the better of him and he reached up to cup her face, holding her still while he took more and more, his lips bruising as he moved over her mouth, swallowing her small whimper. He knew Melissa liked it hard, rough, edgy. The sultry warmth of her breath, the taste of coffee on her lips, it all combined to drive his need higher. He pushed insistently at the seam of her lips until she opened under him, her tongue coming out to rub against his.

Long moments later, he eased away just enough that he could see her face. Her quick little breaths panted over his wet lips. Brilliant green eyes, overwhelmed, a little stunned, stared back at him. He nudged his erection up against her, a slow up and down rub. Her legs parted and he could feel the warmth through their clothes as he nestled closer to her pussy.

"If I don't get you home, baby, I'm going to fuck you. Right here, right now."

"You're as kinky as Richard."

"You don't know the half of it…"

He opened the door and let her slide in before he closed it then walked around to the driver's side. A quick searching look up and down the street while he repositioned his cock so that he could sit down without breaking something and he got in too.

He risked a glance at Melissa. Bad move. She was staring at him intently as if she wanted it. Wanted whatever he did to her. Her hand strayed onto his thigh and sat there, burning through the fabric. Hell, if he was lucky, he'd just make it without having to pull over and take her on the bucket seat. Hands fixed in a tight grip to the steering wheel, he checked the rearview mirror and pulled away.

Five minutes to Melissa's place.

He made it in two and a half.

Chapter Five

Control was overrated. And his loss was apparently tied in with his decision to make Melissa theirs. Or just his, if Richard found for his own reasons he couldn't commit to it.

Spencer had been lurking outside Melissa's flat and the fury that had flared on seeing him had finally lowered to a simmer. He'd never been a man to give in to his emotions easily—his ex-wife would vouch for that—but the minute he laid eyes on Spencer as he bracketed Melissa against the front door with brawny arms, not touching her but definitely invading her personal space, he could easily understand Richard's desire last night to beat the living daylights out of him. The man should just take a fucking hint.

But the effect it had on him was telling. Instead of a man known for his control, he'd acted like the missing link, as though he'd only just crawled out of the cave. If Spencer hadn't backed off and away when he saw Alex coming, Alex would have tossed him into the street without a second thought. Then he'd barely had Melissa inside the door before he had her pushed up against the wall, her legs wrapped around his hips while he ground against her, his mouth on hers kissing her so hard their teeth clicked together.

He knew what he'd been doing—staking his claim, marking his territory, like a bloody Neanderthal.

Just the same, next time he was keeping her with him while he parked the damn car.

He'd taken her to the floor before he managed to wrench his lips away from hers, thankful the rug was soft and thick. Silent, she sat and watched him.

Now that he knew Melissa was safe, the feeling of possessiveness still pulsing through him was almost beyond his ability to deal with. Even in the early days with Cilla when things were new and good and the glow still there, he hadn't felt this way. Which just reinforced his decision that Melissa was the one.

"I'll ask this once, Melissa, and if you say yes, I can't turn away, baby, so be sure. I want you. Do you want me?"

"As much as I want Richard." She nibbled at her bottom lip. "Does that make me a bad person?"

He felt like shouting in triumph. Instead he kept his voice calm. The last thing he wanted was to scare her off. "No, it doesn't." He leaned over and kissed her again. "That makes you perfect. Now take it all off for me. I need you naked."

With a little shiver of anticipation, she shrugged her arms out of her blazer, tossing it to the side. In a blink her top was gone too, showing pale skin flushed a light pink. The soft perfume from her skin hit his olfactory nerve and he inhaled deeply, taking the seductive blend of Melissa's own light vanilla perfume and the soft musky scent of her arousal deep into his lungs. Even her hair shone as a long, wavy lock cascaded over one shoulder to land on her breast, the light brown giving off gold highlights. She was stunning. Lips parted, vibrant eyes watching his every move. And the way she looked at him—wanting him, needing him, *trusting* him—he felt something shift inside him, something fundamental. Something that had been planted nine months ago when they first met. Blooming now into a full flush of desperate need.

Her skirt was next. No panties. Christ. Seeing her sitting there wearing nothing but a lacy bra and a pair of black thigh-high stockings made his mouth water, his cock throb. He wanted to rip his clothes off, blanket her naked body with his own so that nothing stood between them, nothing to stop him taking her over and over again.

He took a deep breath before he dropped down over her. His eyes raked every inch of her body—the hard nipples, the swollen lips of her cunt glistening with her arousal. She was a woman highly aroused, her body ready for her man, for the pounding thrust of his hard cock between her thighs. In his chest, Alex's heart thudded a heavy beat.

With a tug on the lacy cups of her bra, her nipples popped free and his lips covered one, savoring the feel of the tight bud surrounded by silky-soft skin against his tongue. She arched up underneath him as he painted a damp trail across the deep valley in between, repeating the touches on the other one.

Relishing every little whimper, every moan, he sucked and licked his way lower, pausing to swirl his tongue around the dip of her belly then lower still, until he was level with the apex of her thighs.

The smell of her excitement, the lips shining with wetness, all of it was a feast before him.

He sat up, easing her thighs apart until she lay spread before him like a banquet. Running his fingertips up her inner thigh, he watched the giveaway quiver of her muscles.

Moving slowly, he kneeled between her legs, trailing his finger higher until it rimmed the outer lips of her labia. Her juices coated his finger and he lifted it to his nose to sniff and lick at it. Her eyes opened wide as he watched her face.

"Don't move, baby. I've wanted this for months."

Hands holding her legs apart, he leaned down, and with a slow swipe of his tongue, he licked, tasting every inch of her from the juices dampening the lips of her glistening pussy, to the sensitive bud of her clit. Softly, slowly, again and again, he lapped and nibbled at her folds as she writhed underneath him, waiting until she cried out in fretful need before plunging his tongue inside.

He lifted his head when she pumped her hips against his mouth.

"You're moving, when I told you not to."

"Alex!"

Her frustration raised a small smile on his face. "You want me to tie you up? Is that what you're telling me?"

"No, damn it. What I'd like is for you to fuck me, but you aren't getting the message."

"Oh trust me, baby, I'm getting the message, but I'm in control now. Stay still."

Her growl of frustration brought another smile to his lips. He was just getting warmed up…

Replacing his tongue with a finger, he eased it in, stroking gently then leaned over to kiss her, giving her a taste of herself on his tongue. "Don't you taste amazing, baby?" he said when he lifted his head.

Thoroughly soaked by now and coated with her juices, he moved his finger down to the small pucker of her ass. She stiffened as he probed and pushed gently.

He moistened a finger in the spill of her juices again, gathering more and more wetness as he repeated the process. Each time, her body tensed a little less.

"Relax, baby," he soothed. "We've done this before," he reminded her gently as he released the breast he'd been nuzzling and worked the tip of his finger through the tight clench of muscles, pushing gently but firmly against the resistance.

She gasped as he continued to moisten the tight hole and push a little deeper each time. Leaving his finger there, he leaned back down to nibble at her, lapping at her juices before licking up to suck on her clit.

A harsh moan left her mouth and he raised his head to look at her. Her gaze was frantic, needy, and he took that moment to push his finger fully through the snug grip of the sphincter muscles. "Okay?" he asked, waiting for her nod.

He circled his thumb around her clit, rubbing softly, still thrusting a finger slowly into her ass. Her juices trickled down, providing more lubrication so his finger slid in and out easily. Even so, when her muscles gripped his finger, his cock jerked in response. Soon he'd take her there. Maybe with Richard. He ached at the vision of her on her hands and knees, his hands spreading the cheeks as he worked his cock into the reddened hole, sliding in and out and watching as the little pucker flowered open around his shaft.

Her hips began to shift against his palm, her fingernails digging into his shoulders, her body tightening under his. When he bit down gently on the rosy peak of her breast, she let out a long, keening cry, shudders passing through her body, muscles clenching around the base of his finger. It was amazing to watch and a part of him wanted to do it all over just to watch her as she came. But it was past time he got inside her. When she came around his finger, he'd almost spilled himself like a nervous youth.

After she descended from the little climax, he stood and started to undress.

Totally naked, he stroked the length of his cock from base to tip while she watched, spreading the lubricating pearls of pre-come over the head so that he couldn't stifle the moan. "Do you see what you do to me, baby? How hard you make me?"

Her eyes were glassy. She licked her lips.

"Do you want me? Tell me. I want to hear you say it. Say you want me." It was suddenly desperately important that he hear the words telling him what she wanted…that she wanted *him*. When her arms rose up to him and her legs parted further, beckoning him, he felt as though he would never be complete again until he was clamped inside her warmth, sliding into the heated depths of her snug channel.

"Yes, Alex. I want you. Fuck me—*please!*"

Hearing his name, her words whisper across her lips, he released his cock and dropped to his knees between her spread thighs, leaning over her with a hand on either side of her head, holding himself above her. Their eyes locked, the steely blue of a stormy ocean clashing with sunlit green of new spring growth.

"Guide me in, baby."

He inhaled sharply at the touch of her warm hand on his cock, running the flared crown of his shaft over her slick labia before positioning him at the entrance where he paused, his body screaming at him to take her.

"Now?" he asked, fighting to keep his driving hunger in check.

Like a cat with a bowl of cream, she smiled up at him. "Oh yes, definitely now."

God, how could any man resist that?

When he absorbed the light touch of her heels settling on his back, he started. Slowly, without stopping, he slid in his entire length, closing his eyes as the glorious heat surrounded each inch of his erection, gasping with the pleasure until he felt the full sac below his cock slap gently against her buttocks.

Dropping to his elbows, he leaned over to kiss her, at the same time thrusting slowly then withdrawing to the tip before he slid all the way back in.

Her hands came up to clasp his head, her kiss gradually becoming more urgent, small whimpers escaping her mouth to be swallowed up in his with each unhurried shaft of his cock into the depths of her channel.

Lowering his body until the hard buds of her nipples and the warmth of her breasts met his chest, he left her lips, trailing his tongue over the soft skin of her jawline to nibble on her ear, swirling his tongue around the shell, feeling the shiver it sparked throughout her body.

"Do you have any idea how you feel around my cock? Those little muscles sucking at me, gripping me, your juices flowing so freely that even my balls are coated with them, and the heat—when I'm inside, I never want to leave. I want you to burn me, set me on fire... I can't get enough.

"Alex...Alex...Alex..."

"Yes, baby," he groaned as the suck and pull on his cock grew stronger. "Tell me." He held her tossing head in his hands, forcing her to still. "Open your eyes and look at me. Now! Tell me what you want from me..."

With a little moan, she opened her eyes, licking her dry lips. "Make me come, Alex. I can't take much more."

At the sound of her soft, desperate plea, his name barely a sigh on her lips, his heart tripped, unleashing a torrent of emotion. He withdrew, gritting his teeth as his cock scraped along the walls of her sheath. In a quick movement, he flipped her over, positioning her on her hands and knees in front of him.

Christ! As he glanced down to position his cock at the entrance to her cunt, he noticed the shiny trail of her juices running down her inner thigh. With his large hands spanning the silky expanse of her hips to steady her, he sank inside her molten heat on a harsh groan. Releasing a hip, he placed a splayed hand on her back, tilting her forward and down, raising the angle further so he sank the last inch. A ragged growl erupted from deep in his chest and he finally thrust— hard, again and again, feeling the clamping around his cock grow stronger, tighter.

"This sweet pussy is ours, baby, mine and Richard's. Say it. Say it!"

Her back arched, her head tipped back and she panted back at him. "Yes. Oh God, yes."

"Ours! You're ours." Stretching out along the curved line of her back as he supported himself on one arm, he reached underneath their bodies with his free hand and pinched her clit between his fingers.

"Yours! Oh God! Alex!!" The scream was torn from her as her body convulsed beneath his.

Feeling the contractions of her orgasm along the shaft of his cock shattered the remainder of his control and with a powerful surge, he thrust hard, again and again until he came, the intensity of the ejaculations so strong that blackness threatened, and he gulped air in quickly.

Slumping over her, heaving, he shook his head. "God, what you do to me..."

Her arms collapsed and he braced an arm around her waist, supporting her as he lowered her to the floor.

"That...makes...two..." she managed to utter before she sprawled completely on the rug.

"Yeah, sweet baby," he panted, scattering light kisses over her shoulders. "That makes two of us."

When her breathing changed to the steady, soft little pattern of sleep, he reluctantly rolled off her to the side, running a hand down her back and over the soft swell of her buttock. "Ah, sweet Melissa. What are we going to do with you?"

He got up, sitting back on his heels to consider the picture of Melissa spread out before him, the seductive flair from her waist to the fullness of her hips and buttocks, her inner thighs and pussy glistening with their juices... And his heart tipped over.

Even though he felt exhaustion overtaking him too, he scooped her, still sleeping, up off the floor and walked into the bedroom with her snuggled against him.

He pushed back the quilt and laid her down, taking a moment to straighten her bra and place kiss over each nipple. Slipping in beside her, he pulled the comforter over them both, spooning her against him, holding her there with a leg thrown over one of hers, and molded a palm around a full breast before surrendering to the irresistible tug of sleep.

* * * * *

Some sixth sense woke Alex and his eyes snapped open, searching in the darkness for danger.

They landed, not on danger, but on Richard sitting on the end of the bed, still fully clothed, a little damp, watching Melissa. Surely he hadn't been walking in the rain...

"Where the hell have you been?" he whispered.

Richard's head lifted and his expression was heavy. "Sorry." He nodded at Melissa still sleeping soundly. "Looks like you've worn her out. Come out to the living room so we can talk. Let her sleep." He smoothed some wayward strands of hair off her face. "She looks like she needs it."

Alex nodded and scooted out from under the quilt without disturbing Melissa then tucked the quilt back in around her so she wouldn't notice his missing warmth. After pulling the door to, he followed Richard out to the living room.

He turned on a lamp and tossed Richard a rueful grin at the clothes and shoes scattered around the floor. "She has that effect on me."

"Tell me about it," agreed Richard.

"Where have you been?" Alex asked as he sat in a lounge chair, still naked. Cold had never bothered him and he didn't intend being out of bed long enough for it to be a problem. "I thought you said you'd be here by nine. Hell, you didn't..."

"No, I wasn't with anyone else, if that's what you're suggesting." Richard plonked down on the sofa and looked over at him, a haunted look in his blue eyes. "I can't. I'm...this isn't turning out the way I expected...or intended."

"Melissa?"

Richard nodded. "We had a fight today. We both said some things. I guess they've been preying on my mind since. After my final session tonight, I went home. Needed some time alone to think."

"I don't need to ask about what." Alex could read the distress in his friend's eyes. "And?"

"Things are changing between me and Melissa. It started out as fun."

Alex nodded.

"But now...I care about her, Alex. I mean, *really* care about her. And this thing with Barry..." Richard stood and paced, running a hand through his hair.

"Melissa isn't Lanie, Richard."

"I know that!" Richard spun around. "At least my head knows that. But what if something happens and I can't protect her? What if—"

"Look, what happened with Lanie was *not* your fault. It was three against one and they were armed. No one, *no one*, could have done more. Besides, you're jumping the gun. Nothing might happen. And Melissa has both of us. You're not alone this time. Give her a chance, mate."

"The mess with Cilla is mucking up my head too. What if Melissa doesn't want this? I don't want her hurt. Hell, I don't want to go through that again. So I keep wanting to pull back emotionally and I know she doesn't understand why."

"Right now she's confused. And the situation with Barry isn't helping."

Richard's eyes narrowed, his body taut. "Something happened?"

"He was here tonight. When we arrived home. Let's just say he's lucky he's not shitting his teeth. The sneaky bastard never really does anything to warrant it. Oh, he was nice as pie when I walked up. That's the thing—he hasn't actually done anything yet we can take him out for."

"He'll slip up though, and when he does, we'll be there." Richard sat down again, his face set. "Guess that answers my own question. No matter what, I can't walk away from her."

"Just as well, Richard, because when this shit with Barry is over, I intend making things permanent with Melissa. I want it to be the three of us more than anything, but if you feel you can't, I don't think I have the strength to let her go."

"That was fast."

"Not really. I've had a few more months than you to brood on how stupid I was to let her go."

"She sure does that to a man."

They both looked up when the bedroom door opened. A sleepy Melissa walked out pulling her robe around her, brushing her long hair back off her face. "Richard?"

"Hello, love." Richard felt his heavy mood lighten at seeing her.

"Where were you? Are you all right?"

"Yes, I'm fine, puss."

"Fine? That's it?"

Ah hell, he knew that look. His puss was working herself up into a nice little spit.

"What happened to 'if you leave that office before I get there tonight, I'll spank your arse so hard you won't be able to sit down for a week'?"

"Something came up."

"Something came— And of course, you didn't think to phone because, hey, it's just good old Melissa—she'll understand." Her eyes were watering, even if they were shooting sparks at him. "You suck, Rich."

Richard stood and grabbed Melissa around the waist, pulling her close.

Wrenching her body out of his hold, she fisted her hands on her hips and fastened a pair of fiery green eyes on him.

"Look—"

"Maybe if you'd take your safety a bit more seriously, Melissa, I wouldn't have to come down on you like that. Did you think of that?"

"But—"

"Look, enough! Melissa—" Suddenly he didn't want to fight with her. He just wanted to hold her close, be held.

"I was worried about you, you obnoxious, overbearing pain in the—"

Her genuine concern touched him, allowing warmth to filter into the cold places in his heart. She shut up as Richard stalked over to her and for now he was determined to say something to keep her that way. But his words faltered as he looked at her. Captivated by the look of irate indignation on her face. "What I wanted to say…"

"Well spit it out, buster." She glared at him then rolled her eyes, disgruntlement evident in every tense line of her body. "It's the middle of the night, this room is fucking cold, I'm freezing my heinie off and you're lost for words—for once," she muttered.

As he watched her pace and mumble, flicking annoyed glances back at him, he felt the tension leaving his body. From where he was sitting, Alex was sprawled back in the chair, smiling at them. And like that, it fell into place. This was it—this was the woman for them. Their Melissa. The only woman who would stand up to him. Meet him head-on. Make him accountable to someone other than himself. It was a good feeling, a feeling of belonging where he hadn't for so long.

And God, she was beautiful. Emerald eyes flashing fire at him, breasts lifting and lowering in time with the quick little puffs of her breaths.

A different heat filled him. He wanted to feel that fire and passion he knew so well. He moved closer, crowding her against the wall so that her fists quickly unclenched from their position on her hips and moved to flatten on his chest.

Her eyes widened and when her tongue licked her lips nervously, leaving a glistening trail, nothing had ever been as important as tasting that soft, moist flesh.

"Richard…" Her surprise at this turn of events was evident when his name escaped her lips as little more than a breathy moan. He wanted and needed more of that. And he would have it. Tonight.

"Don't speak, puss. Just kiss me. Please."

He wrapped his arms around her, holding her in a tight hug.

Breathing deeply, he inhaled her soft, tantalizing scent and lowered his head until his lips moved over the soft landscape of mouth, licking and nibbling, tasting the exquisite sweetness of her lips. At the first touch she stiffened, but he kept up his steady relentless assault. A feeling of intense satisfaction filled him when she softened against him, a hand sliding from his chest to settle around his neck, pulling her closer.

"Open up," he whispered against her lips. "Let me in."

On a soft breath, her lips parted under his and he groaned against her mouth, hungry to claim as much of her as possible.

Her surrender made him ravenous. He tilted his head, moving his mouth over hers, straining to taste every bit of her, thrusting in and out, over and over again. When her other arm reached around his neck to hold him closer, the primitive side of him rejoiced, roared, howled with triumph. She wanted him. As much as he wanted her. God, how he wanted her. If only he could admit it to her, say the words women needed to hear.

From her response, he knew she would be wet for him. As ready for him as his aching cock was for her.

Breathless, he drew away from the seductive warmth, but only for a moment. Cupping her face with one hand, his thumb stroked the silky skin of her cheek as she trembled against him before trailing down her neck and over the dip and swell of her breasts. He slipped a finger under the fabric of her robe to brush over the turgid nub of a lace-covered nipple.

"You know what I think?" Alex said, his voice deep and husky. "I think it's time for bed."

Melissa looked at the two men and swallowed. "The three of us?"

Alex nodded and walked into the bedroom, leaving them to follow. "If you're nervous, we can give you something to distract you," he said, a teasing look in his eyes.

"Such as?" she asked, feeling the reassuring tightening of Richard's grip on her hand before he let her go. She perched on the edge of the bed.

"Lie down on the bed and you'll find out."

Alex was still naked and also aroused, but her mouth went dry, her heart thumping in her chest as Richard begin to strip. The intense look in his eyes spoke of more than simple sexual arousal. His shirt, almost ripped from his body, went flying. Her mouth dropped open. The view in front of her was nothing she hadn't seen before, singly, but the two of them...*together*?

Both men were broad-shouldered with rippling muscles, but where Richard's chest was smooth, Alex's pectorals were covered with a layer of dark hair, tapering to a vee above his abs to then trail in a line down...and down...until...

Oh my God, she thought as Alex's incredible erection bumped his stomach. Hands on his hips, his dark blue eyes bore into hers and a wicked grin kicked up the corners of his mouth.

Movement caught her attention and she gulped as Richard slowly released the top stud on his jeans, sliding the zipper down, a sexy smile creasing his face as he opened them and jerked his hips at her.

She didn't know what to do, what to say. Her body felt wired with anticipation. But looking at the two most gorgeous men she knew standing there for her, wanting *her*, and a feeling of incredulity rocked her. The knowledge that they were both here, with her, seemed a dream too good to be true.

Richard shucked off his jeans, peeling down his black Jockeys at the same time. The solid thrust of his erection rose up to match Alex's, the flared crown dark and swollen, ropy veins twisting around the thick length.

Wrapping his palm around the shaft, Richard watched her as he started to stroke. "This is for you, Melissa. You know, I can't even be in the same room as you without being so hard I can hardly move. Alex too."

Her eyes followed Richard's over to Alex. He was also stroking. "Now," Alex said, pausing in his slow movements to capture the small drop that leaked from the tip, swallowing a moan as he rubbed it over the head, "start by taking off your robe, baby."

"We want to see everything, Melissa," said Richard. He continued stroking his cock. The tip glistened, making her hunger to taste it. She licked her lips and his hand sped up, becoming harder, faster. A shudder seemed to pass over him and he slowed. "Now strip."

Unable to take her eyes from the picture of these magnificent men standing in front of her, pleasuring themselves for her, she rose to her knees and let go of her robe, shrugging it from her shoulders before tossing it on the floor. A whisper of cool air blew over her skin and she shivered, her nipples beading inside the lacy bra.

"The bra," Richard croaked, his hand stopping its movement to clench in a tight fist around his shaft. His eyes skated over her breasts, his breath coming faster. His guttural "Off!" had her wriggling out of it, letting it drift off the bed to join the robe on the floor. She was left kneeling in just her stockings.

"Those too." Alex held his hand out to help her off the bed.

Bending over, she skimmed each stocking down, sucking in a sharp breath as Richard ran a hand over her bare buttock then leaned down to lick and nip it.

Before she could toss her stockings to join the bra, Alex grabbed them. "For later...in case," he said, and threw her a suggestive wink.

Suddenly she felt nervous, self-conscious. She was realistic enough about her body to know that the likes of *Playboy* would never be knocking on her door. Sure, she had the big boobs, but that just meant they were in proportion to the rest of her, and the rest of her looked as if a visit or two to the gym with Richard wouldn't go astray. So being totally naked in front of two guys with bodies that would make the gods jealous, one of whom was a personal trainer, she felt as if every bit of cellulite and saggy skin was under the spotlight. She reached behind her, curling shaky fingers into the sheet, prepared to give it a good tug off the bed—

"Don't! Leave it!" Alex growled. "You're magnificent, baby. The fullness of your breasts with those tasty nipples. So sensitive. So responsive. And the soft pillow of your belly. The way your pussy lips are plumping as you look at us. The wetness leaking from the slit..."

She was surprised she was the reason for the hunger that slipped into his tone, the look of almost feral satisfaction on his face.

"Now, cup your breasts for us."

She closed her eyes briefly for a moment, firming her resolve, then did as he asked. Both men watched intently as she moved her hands up, cupping the weight in both hands, lifting them as if in offering.

"Your nipples—" Richard's voice sounded rough, tortured. "Pinch them."

A grimace of what she hoped was desire passed over his face as she pinched and twisted the puckered nubs, biting her lip as the sensation spiked in her clit. Richard's hand moved quicker, the strokes more firm.

"I want to touch myself..." She surprised herself by blurting out the admission, but the expression on their faces as they stared at her made her want to do wild things.

Richard nodded sharply once and held his breath, his body rigid, his fingers wrapping tighter around his shaft as he watched her fingers leave one reddened nipple to trail down over the flesh of her belly, dipping briefly into the small depression before raking through the light brown curls below. Then a single finger swiped a line through the moisture that had gathered, leaving her finger glistening with her juices.

Richard groaned as she slipped a finger between the swollen lips and pushed it deep. When that finger left her pussy and she raised it to her mouth...

In one quick step, Richard was at the bed, growling, and she gasped in surprise as his hand shackled her wrist and he sucked her finger into his mouth, licking it, inhaling, savoring the scent of her arousal.

"That sweet cream is all for us, love. Later we might let you tease us that way, but not yet. Not until we've had our fill. Now lie back and spread your legs."

The dominant tone in his voice tossed Melissa into a whirlpool of sensations. As Richard moved between her legs, kneeling in front of her, she realized she'd already lost the battle to hold back, to step slowly into this relationship with the two of them. They could make her do things she'd never do with other men.

Richard ran a finger up and down her pussy, teasing and tormenting her needy channel, spreading the natural lubrication over the folds and circling the sensitive nub at the top before pushing the finger inside. His eyes, darkened to a midnight-blue, flicked up to hers, the heated look he gave her enough to make her pulse skitter like crazy.

He lowered his head between her splayed thighs. A long, slow swipe of his tongue along the silky folds of her pussy had her arching her hips toward him. Then his finger began a steady, slow thrust and withdraw, going a little deeper each time. A second joined the first. Then a third. The fourth stretched her, the bite of pain mixing with the pleasure when his lips and teeth closed over her clit, nibbling and sucking gently on the tender nub.

It was too much. Her hands clenched in the sheet as she strained to get closer, to put an end to the torment he was inflicting on her.

After taking a torturous lick, his tongue swirled around her clit, flicking it, making her body shake with the collision of sensations. But in spite of that, she felt empty, as if she needed more.

"Please. Please…"

"Soon."

And then his tongue thrust into her vagina, licking and plunging deeper.

Already, her body felt on fire, as if every nerve ending were a raw wound, the flesh ultrasensitive. And deeper, where Richard licked and nibbled, a tightening in her womb heralded the onset of her orgasm.

"Yes, love, give it to me."

When his lips closed over the swollen nub of her clit and sucked, her world shattered and she panted her release, long shuddering moans she was helpless to stop.

Her channel still pulsing, her body shaking with the power of her climax, she whimpered as her body was turned until she was on her hands and knees, the head of Richard's cock pushing at the swollen entrance of her pussy.

Alex moved onto the bed until his erect cock was pointing directly at her mouth. She cast a glance up at him, noticing the tight cast to his features before she dropped her head, inhaling deeply of his masculine scent as she swiped her tongue around the crown.

She moaned around Alex's length as Richard worked deeper with short thrusts that buried his cock a little farther each time. The muscles lining her channel, still sensitive from her climax, tightened around him until he was all the way in, filling her. Her eyes blinked open when he didn't move.

Alex looked over at Richard, seeing his fingers clenched tightly over the soft skin of Melissa's hips. The look of pleasure on his friend's face so acute, it was taking all his control to stay still and not pound into her as if she were the last fuck he'd ever have.

God, he knew that feeling. He experienced it every time he saw her naked. Like now.

Alex was fighting his own battle with holding still while Melissa began a detailed exploration of his cock with her tongue. Only excruciating control stopped him from moving when her tongue lapped a slow, damp line down to his scrotum then back up, following the line of his shaft until she reached the crown where a small bead of fluid awaited.

Her slumberous eyes lifted to his, held them transfixed as she licked the drop away, the indolent movement reminding him of a cat. Her pink tongue swirled around the flared head, raking over every screaming nerve ending so his hips jerked against the closed portal of her mouth. Then she was lapping again at his balls, taking one into her mouth and tonguing it gently. He gritted his teeth against the sensation but a small moan escaped. Sweet Christ! What next? What was Richard waiting for? Why the hell didn't he move, give her something to distract her, because this torture was driving him insane.

Her tongue reached the smooth skin under his now-tight sac, stroking the sensitive spot, and he gritted his teeth, his entire body rigid. His cock was leaking, thin beads of clear liquid pulsing weakly as he watched her, transfixed, wondering where she would head next.

Damn! Damn! "Suck it, baby! Don't tease me. Not now."

When her mouth closed over his cock, allowing him to sink into the blessed warmth, it was a relief. His head dropped back and he closed his eyes, relishing the wetness, the incredible sensation of her teasing the ultrasensitive bundle of nerves under the head each time she pulled back.

God, yes.

The rapid thumping of his heart threatened to push it out of his chest.

"Richard! Move!"

Sweat was beaded on Richard's brow, his eyes transfixed on Melissa's mouth swallowing Alex's cock. As he looked up, a dark smile covered his face and he began to pull out slowly then surge back in. Building the speed with each thrust.

Alex's heartbeat raced in his chest like a thoroughbred stretching for the finish line.

Unable to tear his eyes away, Alex watched as her mouth opened wide, taking him deep. Just as he began to sink into the delicious feeling, he felt her shifting, her body moving. His eyes stayed glued to the compelling sight of his shaft being revealed, inch by glistening inch, as she eased back on his cock. As she hummed in time with Richard's thrusts, she sank a finger into her mouth, the moist lips swallowing it, licking it, making it wet.

He stiffened when her glistening finger moved down between his legs, running over the clenching pucker of his anus.

She wouldn't!

Christ!

He gritted his teeth, his legs widening of their own volition.

With a featherlight touch, she swirled her finger around, sending electric pulses through his cock.

"No. Baby, what—"

"Relax, Alex. Let me..."

Relax?

He moaned loud and long when she swallowed his length again, the head of his cock hitting the back of her throat as her cheeks hollowed out and she sucked. And sucked.

"No...oh, fuck yes!"

The teasing finger, remoistened from the juices now running down her thighs, breached the tight hole, nearly sending him off the bed as he arched against her, driving his cock deep until he hit the back of her throat.

Slowly that finger penetrated farther, working in and out in time with the movements of her mouth. With a mind that had come adrift from his body, he became aware of her finger, fully inserted, bending, fondling the small kernel of his prostate.

Combined with the sucking pulls on his cock, his entire body began shaking, anticipating. Building to an intensity he'd never felt before.

It felt as if every cell in his body were pooling in his groin. Fire raced through his blood. His pulse pounded. Sucking in great draughts of air, he fisted his hands in Melissa's hair, readying himself for the explosion accelerating through his body.

She moaned as she deep-throated him, the vibrations traveling down his cock, and when she pressed directly on the spot in his back passage, the combination triggered his volatile orgasm. With a shout, he exploded in her mouth, each pulsing jet seemingly torn from his body. Again and again. He crashed back on the bed, gasping.

With a savage cry, Richard sped up the pistoning of his hips, the slap of flesh on flesh driving both Melissa and Alex higher, his cock deeper into Melissa's mouth. And when Richard stiffened, the heated spurts of his come splashing deep inside, it triggered another climax in Melissa, making her body tremble and shudder with the intensity.

As Richard eased his shiny cock from her, the smell of sex filled the air. He rested his head on her back, panting, and closed his eyes for a moment before leaving the bed and heading into the bathroom. He returned with a washcloth, running it over her pussy, her back, cleaning her so that she could sleep well.

When he returned, he crawled up beside her, pulling her snug against his body so that he spooned around her. "Now sleep, puss. You've worn us out."

She murmured sleepily, a smile on her face, and when her leg hitched up to lie across Alex's body, nestling her damp pussy against his leg, he brought her head down onto his shoulder, laying kisses on her forehead.

"Sweet, sweet Melissa. You're going to be the death of us."

Chapter Six

Melissa floated through the doorway of her office on a cloud of satiated bliss. She was so disgustingly happy, she didn't even care that no one seemed to have remembered her birthday.

But then, prior to this morning, her idea of a perfect wake up was a surprise of breakfast in bed. Instances of which, in her whole life, she could count on one hand.

This morning had forced a serious reassessment on the values of toast and tea on a tray as opposed to Richard planting one of those long, slow, "I don't have time to fuck you, so I'll just make love to your mouth" goodbye kisses on her. With her body still struggling to full consciousness, his kiss had melted every single neuron connecting her body to her brain before he headed out at dawn to meet a client. She'd revived about an hour later to the smell of bacon cooking. Alex had fed her scrambled eggs and bacon, surprising her with his culinary skills, then whisked her into the shower where he'd picked up where Richard left off. It was safe to say she was cleaner than she'd ever been in her whole life. Her body-brain connection was still a bit questionable—she suspected her brain was stuck in stutter mode somewhere between orgasms two and three—and so it was amazing her legs were working.

Niggling at her was the thought that waking up with two men was not normal. But she was feeling so fabulous, the niggle had been downgraded to a *pfft*. Nothing was going to push her off her personal cloud nine.

"It's about time you arrived," said Cynthia. "You're looking happy for a change. Did you get lots of presents this morning? Happy birthday, by the way."

Melissa said nothing but blushed and giggled instead.

Cynthia stood back and eyed Melissa suspiciously. "What's wrong with you? You sick or something?"

"Nope," Melissa said, and grinned some more.

"Right." Cynthia's eyes narrowed. "You got lucky this morning, didn't you. Early morning quickie. You still have sex on the brain."

"Better than breakfast," Melissa said, unable to stop the goofy smile from spreading over her face. "Better than food—period."

"Good grief, I don't think I want to know. Go take that sickening euphoria somewhere where I don't have to watch it, like your office. Which, by the way, is awash in tinsel and bows. From the looks of it, someone remembered your birthday."

"Really? Who're they from?"

"I don't know everything, Melissa. Guess you'll just have to unwrap them and find out. Now that you're here, I'm going to duck out for coffee. Would you like one?"

Hand on the door to her office, Melissa turned back. "Please. Jumbo-sized, double-strong, four sugars."

"That must have been some good morning! You go open your presents. I'll be back in a minute."

A profusion of colors and scents met Melissa when she opened her door. Flowers, lots and lots of flowers, the heavenly fragrance filling the small space, sat on every flat surface. Lillies, roses, sprays of baby's breath, exotic orchids... And on her desk, a small pile of boxes, wrapped in shiny paper tied with ribbons and elaborate pom-pom bows. Although neither Richard nor Alex had mentioned it, she hoped one—or both—of them had remembered.

Happiness filled her as she moved to the flowers, sniffing the delicate scent of a pink rose—her favorite—before putting down her briefcase and looking for a card attached to the bouquet. Nothing. That was odd.

She unwrapped the first gift—a DVD boxed set of movies she'd been meaning to buy for months now. She rustled through the paper then examined the box—again, no card. Perhaps she had a secret admirer.

Ten minutes later she was surrounded by what seemed like her entire wishlist of gifts—books, DVDs, a Prada handbag she'd had her eye on for months, perfume. Even two tickets to see the musical *Symphony*—which was sold out for the next two years—for the 7:30 p.m. showing tomorrow evening at The Palladium.

She sat back in her chair, trying to figure out who the sender could be. Her earlier hope that it could be Richard or Alex, or both, fizzled out. Since neither of them had been in touch with her over the past few months, there was no way they could have known—to this degree—the things she wanted.

So who knew her so well, so...intimately, that he'd catered to every item on her personal wishlist.

She was still puzzling it out when the door to her office opened and Richard walked in, carrying her jumbo-sized coffee. Her confusion faded at the smile on Richard's face as he put the coffee down then walked around her desk to take her hands and pull her out of her chair.

"Hello, love."

"Ah, hi."

She tried to ignore the skittering of sensation as he stroked her cheek, his fingers skimming softly down the side of her face to her neck. Lifting her chin, he lowered his mouth to hers.

The kiss took her unawares—both soft and gentle, lightly brushing, caressing, such a tender touch and incredibly erotic. His other hand joined the first at her neck, tilting her head fully up to him. He tasted so good she didn't want it to end. He pulled away briefly and she inhaled. Richard so close was a heady thing—the smell of his aftershave, the taste of him on her lips. Every time he got so close to her, she just wanted to melt. And he knew it too. The corners of his mouth crinkled as they lifted into a smile. Once more he kissed her, more firmly, moving over her lips, his tongue rubbing sensually against hers. A pinch of her nipple surprised her and her mouth gasped open under his while a sharp shiver of want settled in the apex of her thighs. Richard went deeper, kissing her with an urgency she could only surrender to until she felt fused to him, totally a part of him.

It was a meeting of much more than mouths. When he lifted his head finally, his eyes locked with hers. Emotion swirled deep within them, stronger than lust...the blue tinged with the darker shadow of his need. For *her*. It was an amazing feeling, to be the recipient of that look. She wanted to bask in it forever.

Unable to halt her body's reaction, she snuggled closer, her arms slipping around his neck as he kissed her again, his tongue softly swirling and gently thrusting with hers. He tasted of coffee—rich and strong, addictive—and the subtle scent of his aftershave combined to weave around her senses in a potent mix.

On and on it went—minutes...hours, she didn't know and had ceased to care—his arms moving down to wrap around her and pull her more firmly against his cock, tasting and loving as though it would never end. The feeling so delicious she wanted to climb inside him and never come out.

A warm hand slipped inside her blouse to cup the fullness of a breast, softly plucking at the nipple this time so that a moan escaped before she could stop it.

With a final nip of her bottom lip, he released her mouth, resting his forehead against hers.

"Happy birthday, puss. Why didn't you tell us?"

One mystery solved, she thought. Now she could cross Richard and Alex off her list of potentials. "It's just a birthday. No biggie."

"You still should have told us. We could have made the day special."

More special than the way she'd already begun the day? Not possible.

"Barry?" he asked, looking down at her desk, a small frown creasing his forehead.

She'd considered that briefly, but cancelled Barry off the list. "Um, I don't think so. There's no note. No cards. And really, it couldn't be, Rich."

"Why not?"

"This is the thing. As far as I can recall, none of these presents are things I ever mentioned to Barry. For instance, the boxed set of DVDs—they were only released over the past few months. Same goes for the books—they're all recent releases."

"So, a secret admirer?" He kissed her again, a soft brushing of his lips over hers, the kind that spoke of a sexual and emotional intimacy, almost proprietary. "Should Alex and I be jealous?" her murmured into her ear before he nibbled on the lobe, sending sensation directly to her clit.

That was when it really hit her that for Richard and Alex it was about the three of them. Not Richard and her. Or her and Alex. After last night, it had changed irrevocably to her and Richard *and* Alex.

But how did something like this work? Was it just about the sex, or something more? Did the two men share her equally? Or did one man take precedence? It was hard to believe it would be Richard. And yet...

More and more questions raced through her mind.

"Hey, you okay?"

She answered him honestly. "For a woman who suddenly has two gorgeous men in her life rather than just one? No, not really. I'm feeling more than a bit out of my depth, Rich."

He pulled her against his shoulder and she snuggled into his neck.

"We both love being with you, puss. We both want you. And that means sharing you, caring for you, protecting you." He lifted her head so that he was looking directly at her and his eyes darkened with lust. "I love watching you with Alex. Watching him kiss you, touch you. Bringing you pleasure. It's the same for him." He brushed her lips with his. "It was good last night, wasn't it?"

"It was amazing."

A small smile lightened the intensity in his eyes. "You don't think we're too kinky for you?"

She laughed. "You, I'm not surprised about. I always knew you were. Alex was a bit of a surprise."

"You're okay with it, though?"

Melissa kissed him. "Very okay."

An eyebrow cocked and he tipped his head in the direction of the presents. "So who's our competition? Any ideas? Who've you been dating lately?"

"Me? Dating? Like I've had time or the inclination."

Richard picked up the tickets to *Symphony*. "From the looks of these, somebody is keen on you, love. Box seats, no less. Do you have any idea how hard it is to get tickets to this show?"

"I know, it's sold out. Scalpers?" she offered.

"Perhaps, but then you're looking at some serious money. We're talking a couple of thou—"

Melissa cut him off as a thought occurred to her. "I think I know." She pulled out of Richard's arms and he let her go, somewhat reluctantly. She paced as she thought about it, pulling information out of her head, sorting it.

"You going to share?"

She looked up at him. "Have you heard of FriendsandLovers?"

Richard grinned. "Sounds kinky to me."

"It's an internet dating site, you perv."

"In that case, no."

"Right. Considering your little black book could probably compete with *War and Peace* for size, I guess not."

Richard looked shocked. "God, Melissa, internet dating? Why?"

"Why not? Guys haven't exactly been beating a path to my door. And I was—" She made a move to pack up the gifts on her desk. "Never mind," she mumbled.

Richard grabbed her arm and turned her to face him. "Finish that thought, Melissa. You were what?"

"I was lonely," she said softly.

His expression became so tender she didn't resist when Richard's arms wrapped around her and pulled her close. "Oh love. Come here." He kissed her softly. "Not anymore, puss. Not anymore. Men are silly buggers, you know. Me more than most."

"No argument from me."

He gave her a wry smile. "I thought you might agree with me on that. But no more internet dating for you. We'll do our very best to ensure you're never lonely again."

She shrugged at him. Instead of pushing the point, he frowned and waved his hand over the goodies on her desk. "So, tell me about this lot. Who do you have in mind?"

"A guy I've been corresponding with via email for the past couple of months."

"What makes you think it's him?"

"Information we shared mostly. Trying to find things in common. I think in some of our emails I might have mentioned these things."

"Did you give him your name?"

"Not straight off, but yes, eventually."

"That's a bit risky, isn't it? And your address?"

"Here, yes. Not home. I mentioned once I was trying to locate an early edition of a Jane Austen book. He found it and had it couriered to this office."

"What's his name, Melissa?"

"He goes under JMB online, but his name is Joe. Joe Brown."

"You honestly think that's his real name?" Richard snorted and perched his butt on the edge of her desk. "The question is, what's he after?"

Her eyebrow raised. "Is that a guy thing? Always an ulterior motive?"

"Unfortunately for most men, yes."

"Well hell, I don't know. My track record with men doesn't exactly recommend me for expert status. But I don't think there's anything nefarious in his intentions. He's never even pushed to meet. We email frequently though."

"It seems pretty extravagant for someone you've never even met, don't you think?"

"I got the feeling he's not short of the green stuff."

"That's even more suspicious. If a man's that loaded, usually there'd be no shortage of ladies in his life."

"Anyone ever told you you're a cynic, Richard Danville?"

His mouth kicked up into a grin. "I think you might have—once or twice."

Richard glanced at his watch. "Damn, I better get back to work. I'll be tied up the rest of the day. But call me if you need me. I'll have my phone with me all the time."

The door to Melissa's office opened and Cynthia poked her head in.

"Sorry you two, but your ten o'clock appointment is here, Melissa. And he's in a hurry."

"Oh, okay."

"I'm going." He kissed Melissa briefly, pulled away and then kissed her again, longer this time. He winked at her as he stepped back. "That should tide me over until tonight. Remember," he said as he walked to the door, "call me if you need me. For anything."

"I will. Thanks, Rich."

Melissa sat at her desk and unwrapped the baguette she'd bought three hours ago for lunch. Lunch. *Ha!* she thought to herself as she glanced at her watch. The morning had flown by, but what had happened to the afternoon? It was 3 p.m. and at this rate, she wouldn't be leaving the office until seven. She chewed with relish, the baguette halfway to her mouth for the second bite, and she cursed when the phone rang.

"Hello. Melissa Blake."

"Hey, sweetness."

At the sound of Barry's voice, Melissa had trouble swallowing the rest of her mouthful over the sudden closing of her throat.

"Barry?"

"Who else?"

Who else, indeed.

"What do you want, Barry?"

"Just to wish you a happy birthday."

"Er, thanks."

"You didn't think I'd forget, did you?"

"It hadn't occurred to me, to be honest. It's been a busy day so far."

"I won't hold you up, but I just wanted to make sure the gifts arrived. Are the roses pretty? I know they're your favorite."

Melissa's breath stuck in her throat. Barry was JMB? As much as her mind fought it, and the implications of it, what else could it mean?

Which meant, if that were the case, they'd been corresponding for months now. She'd been telling him things about her life... She felt like kicking herself! God, how could she have been so stupid?

"Melissa?"

"Yes," she gasped, thinking furiously of what to do — how to handle this revelation. "They arrived. But you shouldn't have. Really."

"Actually, that's part of the reason I phoned. I'm going back to Australia, Mel. I thought before I go, you might go to that musical with me. The one I sent the tickets for. To say goodbye properly. Would you do that for me?"

Shit. No, of course she didn't want to go with him. She didn't want to be anywhere near him.

"I don't know if that's wise, Barry."

"One night, Mel. We'll be in public, if that makes you feel better. I'll be good — promise."

From the sounds of it, Barry had finally accepted the reality that it was over between them, which was a relief. Alex and Richard, though, were going to freak when they found out who JMB was. Before she did anything, made any decisions, she needed to discuss this development with them. "Can I get back to you?"

"Need to check with your *boyfriends*?"

The friendly tone he'd been maintaining dropped for an instant and at Barry's slightly snide remark, Melissa felt the heat rise in her face, followed by her ire.

"No, actually, I need to check my calendar with my assistant. Do you have a number I can reach you on?"

With a shaking hand, Melissa jotted down the number. "I'll call you back then. Will tomorrow morning be okay?"

"Sure, sweetness. Sorry if I sounded a bit ticked off. Melissa?"

"Yes?"

"I love you," he said softly. "I always will."

The words were said with such tenderness, such bare emotion, she felt a moment's regret for what could have been. "I'm sorry, Barry."

"Me too, Melissa. Talk to you soon."

Melissa sat with the phone up to her ear for long minutes after Barry had hung up.

Then the full impact of what she'd just discovered, that Barry had been leading her on for months pretending to be someone else, trying to wheedle a way into her life, hit her and the remainder of the regret she'd felt moments ago dried up.

She looked down at her lunch and her stomach revolted.

Susie Charles

Chapter Seven
∞

"So Barry is this JMB you've been corresponding with all this time?" Alex confirmed.

All it had taken was a brief phone call to Richard to tell him Barry was the mysterious sender of the gifts and flowers, and he'd arrived at her office within fifteen minutes to pick her up and take her home. They'd met Alex at her place thirty minutes later.

A cup of hot tea, liberally sweetened with sugar, was slid across the counter in front of her by Richard, and she nodded her thanks before wrapping her hands around the large mug, feeling the warmth filter through her. Melissa looked over at Alex where he leaned against the kitchen doorjamb. "Do you think this is how he found me?" she asked.

"Probably," said Richard. "It was likely the lead, the 'in' he was looking for. You led him directly to you."

She pulled out the barstool and sat down, her legs still shaky, and dropped her head in her hands. "I am so dumb."

"No, love." Richard moved closer to rub a hand up and down her back. "You had no way of knowing."

Her head snapped up and she looked at both of them, noting the serious looks on both their faces. "But why won't he just leave me alone? What will it take?"

"He's obsessed, love. He's not in his right mind."

"Are you sure? Barry can be overly possessive and all, but obsessed? A lot of guys feel that way about their women — I mean, you two can be pretty overwhelming too, but I wouldn't call you 'obsessed'."

"The difference, baby," said Alex, leaving his spot at the doorway to stand in front of her, "is that even though we both love you…" he paused and looked hard at Richard, some sort of unspoken communication passing between them, before catching up her hands and focusing on her again, "we would never try to hold on if you wanted us to let you go. We want whatever you want, whatever makes you happy, and if that isn't us then we'll respect that."

Melissa sat still, her heart racing as she searched Alex's face for the full meaning behind his words. What was he saying? Did he mean that they loved her as friends, or something more? She really hoped it was the latter. Because she was already a goner with the two of them. Even now she couldn't imagine her life without both of them in it.

Richard ran his palm over her head, briefly tangling his fingers in her hair and she leaned into the touch. "Tell her, Alex. She needs to know."

"Know what?" Melissa glanced between the two of them. "Is there something else you're not telling me?"

"Come into the living room." Alex stood and helped her off the barstool, brushing a quick kiss on her forehead and giving her a brief hug. Arm wrapped around her shoulders, he walked her into the living room and sat her down on the sofa. Richard took the cushion beside her, taking her hand in his while Alex paced.

Alex stopped and turned to face her. "I had some of my men do a search of Barry's hotel rooms."

"Hang on…Barry said he's staying at the Dorchester."

"He is, but he also has a room in a small hotel not far from here."

"That's a little…odd." She looked at Richard, noting his serious mien, then back at Alex. "Why would anyone need a room in two different hotels?"

Alex squatted down in front of her. "We have reason to believe he may be planning to abduct you."

"Abduct me? How?"

"You've heard of a Certificate of No Impediment?"

"Sure, when I was at the embassy."

"So you know what it's for. And if I told you that Barry has one made out in both your names?"

"But...but Barry can't marry me without my agreement. It's not possible. It's insane. I don't care what piece of paper he has, I'm not going to say yes."

"Perhaps that's where the drugs come in," suggested Richard.

She went cold all over. "What drugs?" Melissa's head was starting to spin again. That sense of things spiraling out of her control.

"One of my men has been watching over you..." Alex put his hands up to stop her reaction. "Your safety is paramount to Richard and me and we felt it was necessary, so don't bother arguing. Anyway, my man followed Barry yesterday when he left the restaurant to go to that other 'appointment' Richard said he mentioned. You know what roofies are, Melissa? Rohypnol?"

Melissa was shocked. "Of course I do. It's a date-rape drug. But what does that have to do with Barry?"

Alex's face hardened. "He met a dealer and bought some."

Her shock was genuine. "Barry? No, it's not possible. He wouldn't. I mean, he's not a man to give up easily but rape? No, I can't believe it."

"Maybe to him it won't be rape, Melissa," suggested Richard. "Perhaps in Barry's mind he's just taking what he considers his."

"But I'm not a thing. I'm a person. You can't just take a person because you think you own them."

"Think about how things were with you and Barry before you came over here, love. Is it that much of a stretch that Barry would resort to something such as this?"

"That's just plain scary."

"Yes, it is," Alex said. "That's what we mean by him being obsessed. He's not acting rationally. So we need to decide what to do about Barry. It's obvious your little 'fiancés' plan didn't work, even with the added complication for him of not just Richard but me to contend with. He isn't going to just go away."

Melissa could feel the first tendrils of panic starting to rise. "But he told me he's leaving. After the musical. So, in a few days he'll be gone. We just have to wait him out."

Richard ran a hand down her hair, trying to comfort her. "He has no intention of leaving without you, Melissa. Let's get that straight right now."

"So what do we do? Go to the police?"

Alex took a seat in the armchair, his huge bulk filling it. "With what? So far we have nothing that would stick in court. Nothing to arrest him on. The police wouldn't take too kindly to us doing an illegal search of his room, and what's to stop them or Barry from saying we planted the drugs? Besides, he hasn't actually done anything yet."

"If you're going where I think you are, Alex, forget it." Richard's fingers tangled in her hair, tightening, communicating his tension. "We're not putting Melissa at risk like that."

Alex's expression was resolute as he looked back at his friend. "You're forgetting we have a team of highly trained professionals at our disposal. We can protect her, Richard."

"No. Not happening. We'll find some other way."

"How? At least this way we can control the situation, set it up to ensure maximum success —"

"Hang on, guys." She took Richard's hand in hers and squeezed it. "Richard, I know you're concerned for me, and I love you for that, but why don't we at least hear what Alex has to say?"

Richard's expression turned dark. "Fine. I'll listen. But if it places you in any danger, the answer is no."

"Agreed," said Alex. "Here are my thoughts so far. I have a couple of favors I can call in and can probably get a couple of my people into the theatre where *Symphony* is playing, posing as employees. And if I pull in enough of my guys to cover all the exits, there's little to no chance of him getting away."

"It's the 'little' that concerns me," growled Richard. "How can we reduce it to none?"

* * * * *

Stacking the plates and the takeaway food containers, Melissa picked up the pile and walked into the kitchen leaving Alex and Richard to hash it out. The two of them had been going over the details for three hours and she'd had enough.

Richard was less than happy about the plan for Melissa to attend the musical with Barry. In fact, he was royally pissed off. Melissa wasn't too comfortable with it herself. But she could see Alex's point—that it was time to go on the offensive, instead of being on the defensive, not knowing what was coming next or when. So they were going to take the "game" to Barry. At least that way they could be in control, be prepared.

But even with all the safeguards Alex was incorporating to satisfy Richard, there were still unknown variables that could come into it that no amount of planning could accommodate. That was where Richard was currently butting heads with Alex. He wanted every possible scenario considered and then some, fine tuning, working out alternatives, back up plans. And while Alex was being very patient, even she could see they could only plan and anticipate so far.

She washed the dishes, put the empty food containers outside in the garbage bin and then walked into the bathroom to take a shower. It was a bad sign, she supposed, that no one came through to interrupt her bathing, a propensity both Alex and Richard seemed to share. She noticed the razor sitting on the edge of the bath—perhaps a little surprise was what she needed to get their attention.

Ten minutes later, towel wrapped around her, she sat on the bed. Intimate memories of sharing it with both Richard and Alex flashed in an erotic montage through her mind.

But after the showdown with Barry, what then? Once Barry was gone and she was safe, would there be any reason for the men to stay with her?

Perhaps it was the slant the talk had taken but she couldn't shake the feeling of something terrible about to happen, a climax being reached. And she couldn't see beyond it. Apart from Alex's earlier mention of them loving her, which certainly couldn't be construed as a declaration of intent to take things further between them all, there was nothing to suggest they wouldn't just pick up their lives where they'd left off before all this began.

It wasn't as if she hadn't been on her own before. She was a modern woman—capable of having a full life without needing a man to feel complete. What she'd realized though, was that it wasn't about *needing* a man, but desperately *wanting* the two who'd come to mean more to her than just good friends.

But did they want her the same way? And how would that work, anyway? Hell, she'd had enough problems working out one man-one woman relationships. How on earth did one manage *two* men? And if she had to choose, how could she without a piece of her heart always belonging to the one who had to walk away?

Maybe she needed to let them know what *she* wanted for a change. And that meant both of them. Which meant it was she who would have to take the initiative.

She stood, a plan—albeit a little flimsy—forming in her head.

Decided and determined, she dropped the towel.

A little uncomfortable with what she was about to do, she took a deep breath to fortify herself and still her nerves, then walked out into the living room completely naked. The air was cool on her body. Her nipples beaded, a light flush of goose bumps skating over her exposed flesh. She waited nervously, though she attempted to look relaxed, until the men stopped talking and noticed her.

Since she was directly in his line of vision, Alex saw her first, his eyes darkening, becoming heavy with lust. He rose from the seat, his movement slow and measured, almost predatory, until he reached his full height. With his eyes darkening, his nostrils flaring, his entire body taut, he looked like a wild animal about to pounce. His tension must have communicated to Richard because his head snapped around, his eyes widening as he stood too.

With them both standing there staring at her, not speaking, their intimidating presence filled her small room. For one of the few times in her life, she felt small, petite against their solid bulk and height.

"I'm going to bed." Her throat felt dry, but she refused to cough to relieve it and broadcast her nervousness. So her words came out unintentionally husky. Which was probably a good thing judging from the flashes of heat that covered both their faces. "I didn't want to interrupt, but would you mind turning off the lights and locking up after yourselves when you leave?"

Alex watched her closely, his eyes traveling over her body and locking on the soft, silky skin of her now-hairless pussy.

Beside him Richard stiffened, his tone deep and disbelieving, "When we *leave*? You teasing us, puss? Because this is not a good night to tease."

Damn right, thought Alex. With the specter of Spencer hanging over their heads and the potential for danger to Melissa they'd been working all night to minimize, he and Richard were wired and primed for battle. It was a well-known fact that war and sex went together, the release that came with hard fucking often the only thing that could bring a soldier down from the battle high. It was primitive, primordial, but it was the way they were, and when it involved a woman a soldier had strong feelings for, the need to protect her morphed into a possessive compulsion that could only be assuaged by long, hard sex.

And that innocent little look with the wide eyes Melissa was throwing them wasn't cutting it. Her overt display was on a par with a cuddly little rabbit walking into a den of starving wolves. He had a strong suspicion she knew exactly what she was doing and where it would end. Which was fine and dandy with him—he'd had enough talking to last him a week.

Melissa's breath caught in her throat as Alex grabbed the front of his shirt and ripped it apart, sending buttons flying. Hands on his hips, holding the two halves of his shirt open, he watched her eyes skim over his chest then drop lower to where he knew the solid thrust of his erection pressed against his trousers.

"Come over here, baby. You're not going to bed without giving us a goodnight kiss, surely?"

"One kiss?" She walked over to him.

He couldn't tear his eyes away from the slow trickle of moisture that escaped her pussy, dampening her inner thighs as well as making the freshly denuded flesh of her labia glisten. The thought of running his tongue over it, feeling that pretty cunt so soft and smooth under his lips, shot a bolt of lust through him and his dick responded, swelling to capacity between one heartbeat and the next.

"That's all it takes?" She raised an eyebrow as she reached him. "You're easily pleased."

"On my cock," Alex said, and smiled darkly. Her eyes widened at his dominant tone. "Undo my pants."

Keeping her eyes on him, she slid the zipper on his fly down, which wasn't an easy task considering the pistol he was currently packing.

"Take them off as you go," he said.

Since he'd removed his socks and shoes before dinner, there was no impediment to her sliding his trousers down. When they pooled at his ankles, he kicked them away. "And the rest."

His dark blue boxers were next. But when her hand ran up the length of his erection through the silky fabric, he growled and snapped his hand down to cover hers, pressing it hard against his cock, massaging the trapped shaft. The heat of it seared through them both. Taking her hand, he dipped it under the elasticized waistband until her hand was filled with his hot, steely hardness.

"Hmmm, that's good. So good." Alex let her hand go. "Now take them off and get your mouth around it, baby. Fast."

He could just picture the wetness sliding from her pussy at his commanding attitude. It was a recent discovery—her reaction to dominance—that he fully intended to explore in much more depth when they had the time.

As she began to move to her knees, his fingers around her arm stopped her.

"Nu-uh, baby. Bend over and take it."

She started as the implication of her position hit her, how it would leave her exposed to Richard. He grinned as a small whimper left her mouth.

Behind Melissa, Alex could see Richard hurriedly stripping off the last of his clothes. From the look of carnal intent written all over Richard's face, he was being driven by the same protective, possessive demons riding Alex. Tonight wasn't just about a three-way fuck—tonight they were going to claim sweet Melissa as theirs.

As if to put actions to his thoughts, the second Melissa bent over, Richard glanced briefly at Alex, a dark smile on his face, and covered her hips with his hands, moving them to the beautifully curved cheeks of her buttocks, parting them so that he could begin a slow slide of his erection up and down the crevice.

Looking down at Melissa, Alex grasped her head in his big hands, tangling his fingers in her hair until she felt the little pinch of pain he knew would drive the intensity higher. When her lashes began to flutter and she licked her lips quickly, he could see she was ready. He pulled her mouth closer to the softly pulsing head of his cock. "Open wide, baby."

He was a big man—all over—and there'd been a fair number of women were a little disconcerted when they saw him erect. For some, total panic set in when oral sex came into the picture, and they wrapped their hands around so much of his shaft, gripping it so hard they almost cut off the circulation, that the most he got was a good head washing. He'd learned to live with it.

But not their Melissa. Instead she braced her hands on his hips rather than grasping his cock, and he recognized the trust she was placing in him to control the depth of his penetration. If anything, it made him burn more. Her eyes fluttered shut when she eased her lips over his erection, her mouth taking more and more until the inches slid and sank further down her throat. As the heat and wetness surrounded him like a glove, he gritted his teeth so hard against the urgent need to thrust, he swore he could feel bones cracking in his jaw. Alex's eyes shot to Richard. Melissa pulled back, teeth scraping over sensitive nerve endings until her tongue flicked out to lick at the head, and he groaned from deep in his chest. Sucking in a deep breath, he nodded at Richard. *Let's do it.*

Licking the whole of his shaft, nibbling up the length until she reached the crown, she paused, her hot breath washing over it.

"Don't tease, baby. Suck it. You love it, don't you?" God, he hoped so because he had plans for her mouth that would last him the rest of their lives.

With her tongue swirling around the tip, flicking over the ridge of nerves on the underside of the crown, she raised her eyes to meet his, nodding and moaning as she slowly slid down again. He could picture the sweet cream flowing out of her cunt.

He felt her relax her throat so he could go deeper. Grunted as she took him all the way inside so the head nudged the back of her throat.

He held her head in trembling hands, his hips making small jerks. "Yes. Like that. Oh baby!"

Her tongue, her mouth, that wonderful cavern of heat and wetness, sucked at him, sending streaks of fire down the length of his cock to the tight sac beneath.

Richard had crouched down behind her, forcing her legs wider apart. The hum of her pleasure as he began to suck and lick at her vibrated down the length of Alex's erection buried deep in her throat, and when she looked up at him, her lids were heavy.

As Richard's nips and licks became harder, more voracious, her hips began to lift and jerk, muffled grunts and whimpers bubbling up to travel through to Alex. Sparks of indescribable pleasure flowed through his body, centering in the head of his cock, until all he could think about, all he understood, was that he was about to explode.

Not yet! Christ, no. He eased her away and wrapped his hand around his cock, high up the shaft so she could only suckle the head.

Richard rose, his mouth damp from Melissa's pussy, and Alex watched as Richard lifted a finger liberally coated with her juices and began to prepare her for them both taking her. She flinched, her lips closed tight around his cock as that finger worked deeper and deeper into her anus, pushing past reluctant muscles until she relaxed and the second knuckle disappeared, swallowed up in her tight hole. Alex let go of his cock and she filled her mouth with his length.

Watching that finger disappear, followed by Richard's shaky, "Fucking hell, puss!" nearly made Alex blow.

Two quick slaps on her buttocks had Melissa stiffening, her teeth biting down on Alex's cock, not enough to hurt, but the brief spike of pain shot straight to his balls and he had to pull back quickly, his hand gripping his shaft hard at the base to stop the boiling flow of semen from shooting out the head.

Whatever Richard was doing must have felt fucking good because she began to push her hips back against him, slipping her mouth down over Alex's cock again with a long hum.

Richard's other hand slipped underneath Melissa's body, his finger still pumping in and out of her anus, and on a cry around Alex's shaft, Melissa's body stiffened, her lips closing around him like a vise as her body began to shake and jerk.

As the orgasm took her, Alex tightened his fingers in her hair, his jaw bunching with the control it took not to thrust into her mouth.

Richard pulled out of her arse and, with a look of almost feral pleasure on his face, glanced down and placed the tip of his cock against Melissa's pussy, watching as just the flared head was swallowed up in her warmth and wetness.

Taking a deep breath and fighting not to thrust hard, Richard gritted his teeth, his breaths becoming quick pants.

Tearing his eyes away from what Alex knew was the indescribable vision of her pussy lips stretched tight around the head of his cock, Richard looked over at Alex. The same hunger, the same need to bind them together that Alex was feeling was written all over Richard's face. When Richard silently mouthed the word "Now" at him, Alex surrendered his control, and with a growl and a curse, he slid the last couple of inches down Melissa's throat until the curls spiraling around the base of his cock met the soft skin of her lips. Exquisite arcs of electricity shot through him, radiating out from the sensitive shaft, warm threads of pleasure traveling up his back, clenching his buttocks as he thrust and withdrew, thrust and withdrew...

There was no fighting it. No fighting how she made him feel. His hold on her tightening, he steadied her against Richard's powerful thrusts.

"Yes, oh fuck, yes! Now. Now!"

It felt as though Alex hung on the peak forever, that exquisite moment just prior to coming when he felt as though he were balancing on the edge of a cliff, his cock thickening, his testicles drawn up tight. Melissa eased off her fast sucking, her hand grasping him to tighten at the base. Nothing could have driven him more insane. Grabbing handfuls of hair, he strained against her, thrusting as much of his dick into her mouth as she allowed. Withdrawing slowly until just the head was covered, her teeth softly grating the sensitive flesh, he slid back in, feeling her tongue swirl around and around. Fuck! As Richard roared out his climax, the knowledge that hot come was shooting deep inside her made Alex wild and he finally let go, creamy jets of semen pulsing down Melissa's throat in time with the pull and drag of her mouth.

Gulping in air, Alex waited until he was sure his heart was back in his chest and not about to burst out the top of his head. Richard slid out, bending over to kiss up her spine. Then Alex stood her upright, hands clenched on her shoulders. "You're so perfect, baby." And he kissed her roughly, tasting himself on her lips, in her mouth.

Watching Melissa in Alex's arms, her body limp and submissive against his, freed something inside Richard and a proprietary growl escaped before he could stop it.

Melissa broke away from Alex, rolling her eyes at the sound Richard made. "You want more, tiger?"

With a laugh and a shake of her head, she turned to walk toward the bedroom, the smooth mounds of her ass jiggling with each step. A snarl rumbled out of Richard's chest and before she'd taken more than a step or two, he pounced, spinning her around roughly, angling his lips over hers until she was panting into his mouth.

Lifting her easily, he cupped his hands under the silky swell of her buttocks, squeezing and kneading the flesh. His eyes locked with hers. The desire he saw in them just inflamed him more, making him burn. He felt a brief flare of satisfaction when her hands wrapped around his neck, holding her in place. Grabbing the thigh of first one leg and then the other, he wrapped her legs around his hips.

The heat of her bare sex burned his cock. He needed to thrust into that moistness again, feel it grip every inch of his shaft. And stay there. Forever.

A predatory grin creased his face. "Oh, there's more coming, puss. We've barely begun."

Her smile widened. "If you two think you've got what it takes…"

She wriggled until he let her down, then turned and bolted to the bedroom with a laugh. He glanced at Alex and together they moved toward her relentlessly. Stalking her, their expressions determined, hungry. Insatiable.

When Richard raised an eyebrow at her, Melissa knew she was in trouble. He could see it written all over her face. She bit her lip at the look he gave her as he continued stalking toward her.

She laughed and ducked around the bed, looking about quickly to try to decide where to run next. She feinted right, but instead he dived across the bed, shackling her and holding her fast.

Before she knew could say a word, she was face down across his lap, her bare cheeks propped up like two overripe peaches. Richard could feel her juices trickling down between her legs.

"Richard!" She struggled, but he pushed down on her back with one hand while the other one sent soft caressing strokes over the quivering curves of her arse.

"Do you know how much I love this beautiful arse, puss? I have fantasies about biting and licking it. All day. Do you know how awkward it is for me to work with a hard-on just from thinking about it?" A finger slipped down the split in her cheeks, teasing at the wetness, easing, with a soft push, up against the pucker of her anus.

She moaned.

"You want more?"

"Yes!"

"And we will, puss, but first..."

"What—"

Smack!

"You must promise us—"

Smack!

"From now on—

Smack!

"You—

Smack!

"—belong—

Smack!

"—to us."

"Hey!" she panted out, letting out a whimper.

"Promise us, love."

With a gentle touch he soothed the burn away. As she settled under his palm, her breaths panting in and out, he eased two fingers into her moisture-slick channel. Her back arched and her arse rose. A single thrust, buried deep, was all it took.

"I promise. I promise. I belong to you two. I do," she panted. "I belong to you."

"Good girl. Now climb on top of Alex. See, love? He's ready for you."

Alex was stretched out on the bed, watching them, his erection rearing up over his stomach. The thought that soon they'd both be fucking her made her tummy flutter, her breathing escalate. The scrape of the drawer on her bedside table had Melissa looking around in time to see Richard watching her with an intense expression as he retrieved the tube of lubricant she kept there. Melissa scrambled to obey and lowered herself over Alex's groin.

"Will this hurt?" she couldn't help asking.

Richard's warm lips kissed over her inflamed buttocks, licking a soothing path over each one then up her back until his mouth was level with her ear. "We'll never hurt you, love. Trust us to always look after you."

"Always, baby," agreed Alex.

Then Richard moved away and she could feel his hands running soothing circles over her skin until she wanted to squirm.

Alex cupped her face in his strong but gentle hands. There was the same hunger, the same driving need she'd glimpsed earlier, not only in his face, but in Richard's. But now she felt it too. The need to complete what they'd begun. To seal the bond between them.

The looks on their faces told her there'd be no more waiting. No pretty words. This fiery connection they were sharing had gone beyond that.

Her imagination had gone wild since that night in her kitchen, picturing the three of them like this, wondering how it would happen, and her thighs tightened around Alex as she felt Richard settle behind her, his hands warm as they cupped her shoulders.

A hand came around to flick her clit, milk the hard bud until she wanted to cry out. She leaned over Alex, her breaths panting in and out of her mouth, making her lips dry. She licked them to moisten them.

Alex's eyes flared as he watched, before his guttural "Fuck!" startled her, and he grabbed her head, bringing his large body up to meet her. He took her mouth roughly, until she moaned against him and he thrust his tongue inside her mouth.

Her heart pounded when she felt the searing burn of Alex's erection prod at her sex. Two short thrusts and then, with a low groan, he plowed deep, grunting as he buried the long, thick shaft fully in the depths of her vagina.

Nerve endings screamed at the rough treatment, but her body relaxed into his, relishing his hunger, his demand for what he was taking from her.

"Hold her, Alex. Fuck, hold her tight." Richard's rough growl set her further on fire. A lubricated finger prodded at her anus, circling twice before it pushed in. The small burn this time was nothing, quickly consumed by the need for more. She pushed her hips back against Richard's finger, scraping over the length of Alex's cock.

"Just do it, Richard," Alex gritted out then growled at her, "Christ, baby, you're going to fucking kill me."

Melissa was panting. Anticipation of the moment she'd been waiting for roiled through her. Underneath her, Alex held himself rigid, his body taut.

Another finger joined the first and Richard leaned over her, his breath warm as it blew over her ear. "You want this, love? Tell us you want what we can give you."

"I do. Please, Richard."

"Do you burn for us, puss? Only us?"

"Fuck, yes," she panted.

She arched as Richard's fingers slid in deep, pistoning in and out, making her thrust harder onto Alex's cock. "Rich..." she gasped, staring down at Alex. "Now—please—do it...do it... Tell him, Alex."

"Jesus Christ, Richard. Get inside her. Now!"

She moaned as Richard's fingers slid out. The pause was brief and then the sensation was back. But this time it was thicker, harder. Hotter. Burning as the hard shaft pushed against the muscles fighting the intrusion. She wanted it more than she'd ever wanted anything. The feeling of completion, of total possession, she knew was coming.

"Yes! Yes!"

A loud grunt left Richard's lips as the broad head finally breached the sphincter and his well-greased cock slid in until half his length was swallowed up.

"Christ, you're so tight. Melissa...oh fuck, I want you so much."

"Do it!" She couldn't wait, the slow thrusts destroying her. With a yell, she pushed back against him, gasping as she fought to take his full length.

"Hey, baby, relax, come on, let us do the work."

A hand was smoothing over her face, pushing her hair back, and she opened her eyes, not even realizing they'd been clenched shut, to find Alex looking up at her with a combination of concern and dark hunger etched into the lines on his face. His forehead was sweating. The skin under her hands, she noticed, was covered in a sheen of moisture as well.

"Take me," she whispered on a ragged breath.

Strong fingers, Alex's, dug into her hips as he began to stroke. Richard's hands reached around to cup her breasts, fingers tweaking the nipples so the sizzle of sensation arced directly to her clit. She fought to take a breath as a morass of emotions swamped her.

She whimpered as Alex latched on to one of her nipples, being held steady for him by Richard. It was one of the most carnal sights she'd seen.

Richard began to move too, filling her, stretching her, thrusting in counterpoint to Alex, and her breath lodged in her throat.

"Oh Jesus. Oh Christ. She's so tight, Alex... Hell!"

She didn't hear the rest, focused instead on the feel of two cocks plundering her, claiming her, and the drumbeat of her pulse as it pounded out of control.

Alex pulled out and Richard slammed deep, covering her back as he began to piston in and out. All her senses were so acute, so alive, she could feel the two cocks begin to pulse as the tempo increased.

Without warning, her climax exploded and began to tear through her. And when she would have pushed back against Richard, desperate to do anything to prolong the pleasure, a deep growl at her ear stopped her.

His fingers pinched at her clit again, milking it as she screamed, her body arching in their hands as a longer, stronger orgasm burst through her, shattering her mind with a pleasure so overwhelming it was almost pain.

Vaguely she was aware of Alex grunting underneath her, his body pumping inside hers fast and furious. And Richard, big hands clasping her shoulders from behind as he stiffened and yelled out, coming hard.

Hands moved over her back, stroking, caressing, soothing her body as the tremors finally eased. Unable to hold herself up any longer, she slumped down onto Alex's chest. Her beleaguered senses surrendered. Exhausted to the marrow of her bones, she gave up and allowed sleep to claim her.

Chapter Eight

The van was parked a street away from the theatre—the closest spot available—in a disabled parking bay on Great Marlborough Street. It wasn't right outside—the obvious preference—but still within easy running distance, which was the best they could hope for.

In the dim red lighting of the control van, Alex checked the multi-camera display on the monitors covering as much of the exteriors of the theatre as possible before speaking into his comm. unit. "Noel, do you have visual?"

"Aye. Lookin' pretty as a picture, she is. Hang on..."

Alex waited impatiently while a faint hum filled the silence. He was grateful Melissa had been able to talk Barry into meeting at the theatre rather than him picking her up. At least it had given them the opportunity to get properly set up and the team in place.

After a few minutes that seemed like hours, Richard sitting beside him asked, "Something wrong?"

"Don't know. Just waiting on Noel—"

"Sir?"

"Yes, go ahead."

"Sorry. The lady left the box for a few minutes. I'm guessing she ducked out to powder her nose since the curtain goes up in a few."

"Did Spencer go with her?"

"No. Stayed in the box the whole time."

"How is Miss Blake holding up?"

"Fine. Light conversation with Spencer, but that's all. A bit hard to see from this angle, and the lights in their box have been dimmed."

"Ask him how close he's sitting?" whispered Richard.

Alex rolled his eyes at Richard. "How close is Spencer sitting to Miss Blake, Noel?"

"Bit less than arm's length away."

"Good. Keep us posted."

"Will do."

Alex contacted the rest of his team. He'd called in all ten men and the sole woman who were currently on English soil awaiting reassignment. Every exit of the theatre was covered and apart from Noel sitting in a box diagonally opposite and down one level to the one Barry had booked, they had managed to get one man working inside the theatre as an usher.

He turned to Richard. "Apparently Melissa left the box for a few minutes before the curtain. Spencer stayed in his seat. And now we wait." Alex retrieved a two-way earpiece from the desk. "Take this. Put it on. Just in case."

As Richard adjusted the earpiece around his ear, he asked, "How'd you manage to get Noel in there?"

Alex grinned. "It's not what you know…"

"Right. More to the point, how'd you manage to convince him to sit in there for the whole show?"

Noel had served with both of them in the SAS for a five-year period before he'd been discharged on medical grounds. And they both knew that *Symphony* was definitely not his style of musical—his idea of music appreciation ranged from maudlin Irish pub ballads to Hank Williams.

"I promised him a one-week holiday in County Clare. He can wail his heart out in the local pub to his heart's content."

Richard forced a tight grin and nodded. "So now we wait."

"And wait..." Alex checked his watch. The tension was getting to both of them, but more so to Richard. Alex could understand his tenseness. Personally, he'd be glad when the night was over and they could take Melissa home. "Intermission will be at 20:45. If Barry is going to make a move, chances are it will be then."

Richard scanned the monitors again without saying a word.

* * * * *

"Is it possible we were wrong?" Alex asked Richard.

"About Spencer? I doubt it," said Richard. And that disturbed him, making him frown. "What have we missed?"

Intermission had passed with no action. Melissa and Spencer had stayed in the box, not even stepping out for drinks. The show was due to finish in fifteen minutes.

"Nothing," said Alex. "We've checked and triple checked. No exits. Nothing unusual. Melissa is still in place."

At least she was safe—for now. "Let's just hope that holds then. I can't shake this feeling that something is decidedly smelly about this whole setup."

"I know."

For that reason, they'd insisted Melissa wear a discreet tracking unit strapped to her thigh. A final backup, just in case.

Silence reigned between the two for a few minutes before Alex sat up straight, his body going into alert mode. He flicked a switch on the console so the transmission would come through Richard's earpiece as well.

"Movement of the target, sir," came Noel's voice through the comm. unit. "Lady still in place. Pursue?"

"Yes. This could be it. Go, go!"

Richard tensed. "If he's just going to take a leak, I may go in there and cut the bugger's dick off for what he's put us through—"

He broke off as Noel came through again.

"Target heading out the Ramillies Place entrance. Alone."

"Got it. Mark?" Alex waited a second for the response. "Coming your way. Target alone. Follow at a distance. Maintain visual."

"Copy that," said Mark.

"Why the hell would he duck out like that so close to the end and leave Melissa sitting on her own?" queried Richard.

"No idea—"

"Sir?" Noel cut in, panting lightly.

"Go ahead."

"Just checked the box. Miss Blake's gone now too. You want me to check the ladies' room?"

"Shit! Yes," Alex barked out. "Barge in if you have to."

Three minutes and fifteen seconds later Noel was back. "Sorry—had to work my way through a crowd of antsy females to get in there. But she's not in there. No sign of her. None of them had seen a woman meeting her description either."

"Well look around, Noel. Keep your eyes open in case she's on her way out."

"Aye."

"Let's go," rumbled Richard. "We're doing no damn good in here."

On their way out, Alex patted Chris' shoulder as he sat in the driver's seat of the van. "Start the motor and keep it running. If she comes back here, let us know straight away."

Fear for Melissa burned like acid in Richard's gut. But sticking to the plan they'd decided on if things reached this point, he and Alex split up, moving to cover different exits from the theatre, watching with Alex's team for Melissa to come out.

They'd stressed to her repeatedly before letting her go, that if there was no danger, to wait until the foyer of the theatre was nearly clear before exiting down the front steps. The last thing they wanted was to lose her in the crowd.

But when the last of the theatre patrons had dribbled out and a few of Alex's team had gone in to double-check for her, it was time to admit they'd failed her, and she was gone.

"Shit! Shit, shit!" Richard raged.

"Richard!" Alex yelled in Richard's earpiece. "Back to the van. We can track her."

He headed there at a sprint, arriving in time to see Alex nearly drag the side door off its hinges as he opened it with a hard yank.

Alex sat quickly in front of the console and keyed in the password to access the tracking system.

"Fucking Christ!" he said, and banged a closed fist on the desk.

Richard felt the start of full fear building. "We've lost her, haven't we?"

Alex was still tapping at the console. "Spencer must have found the device. It's still showing her as being in the theatre." He stopped and yelled into his comm. unit. "Ralph, Lillian, Francis—inside. Search that place for the tracking unit. Turn the place upside down if you have to. The rest of you, meet back here at the van. Pronto—" He broke off as his phone rang. "Yes?" Alex listened, his expression turning thunderous. "Okay, get back here, Mark. Nothing more you can do there."

He looked over at Richard, his face full of the same helpless fury Richard was feeling.

"That was Mark. He lost Barry somewhere in St. John's Wood."

"Well, a great lot of fucking good that was!"

Alex's frown turned dark, worry etching deep lines in his face, but his voice was even, his words measured, his mind racing ahead. "He's one of my best, Richard. I think it's fairly safe to say Barry's had professional help in this, and that means somebody very good, which also means someone who's expensive. So, contacts. Call anyone you can think of who might have heard of something of this nature going down. Any lead, no matter how small. Let's meet at my office in an hour."

* * * * *

Alex watched Richard pace. He'd been doing it since he arrived and showed no signs of letting up. It was now three hours—as far as they could ascertain—since Melissa had been taken. They'd concluded that the "Melissa" Noel had been watching in the box was a substitute, but so far no one had been able to come up with any workable scenarios for kidnapping a woman from a sold-out theatre without somebody noticing *something* odd.

Most of the team sat around talking quietly. The rest, anticipating an all-nighter, lightly napped while they could.

Everyone snapped to attention when Alex's phone rang and he pressed the speaker key to answer the call, allowing them all to hear.

"Alex Ryan."

"Hello, Ryan. It's been a while."

"Who is this?" queried Alex. The Irish-accented voice sounded vaguely familiar.

"I believe y'know me best as The Wraith. Quaint little title the press have lumbered me with, but it'll do."

Alex remembered him. Too well. The man fitted his nickname. A paid killer and mercenary, he was as elusive as a mist and as shadowy and insubstantial as a ghost. To this day no one knew his real name. They'd butted heads on a job in Darfur when Alex's business was still in the fledgling stages. And while Alex didn't agree with the man's "do anything for money" ethics, he had a very healthy respect for his abilities just the same. He'd be a fool not to.

"I remember you. What can I do for you?"

"More to the point, what can I do for *you*?"

"Talk. I'm listening."

"If ya want the address of your woman, one hundred thousand pounds into me account within the hour."

Richard let out a soft growl and Alex glared at him before replying. "What guarantee do I have that you'll deliver?"

The Wraith tsked. "Ryan… You're just wasting valuable time, man."

"Were you behind the abduction?"

"I was. Were ya impressed? Ya gonna offer me a job?"

Alex could hear the humor in the man's voice and ignored the obvious bait. "Why? Why give us the address?"

The Wraith snorted. "Because the man bought me expertise not me loyalty. Besides, even in spite of me…*reputation*, there are two things I can't countenance—drugs or rape. I won't dirty me hands with either."

"How much did Spencer pay you?" asked Alex.

"A quarter of a million."

"So if you do have some ethics, why charge us too?"

"Business, Ryan. Purely business. Take down this account number…"

Alex scribbled a line of numbers. "And?"

"I'll call ya the minute it shows up in me account with the information you'll be wanting."

"Wraith?" Alex cut in before the man could hang up.

"Last freebie, Ryan. What is it?"

"Has Spencer raped her?"

"Spencer's not in this for sexual kicks, Ryan, so I doubt he's going to do a thing until the damn drug he pumped into her wears off. He wants your woman conscious and aware. So, time's ticking away. Whether he has the chance or not is up to you now, isn't it? The sooner I get that transfer, the sooner you get the address."

As soon as the call disconnected, Alex booted up his laptop. While he waited, he looked at Richard. "Cheap at half the price. I would have expected more."

Within minutes Alex had logged on to his account, and without batting an eye, transferred the money over.

Fifteen minutes later, he had an address in Dover.

"Okay, boys and girl, let's move it."

* * * * *

Lighting the last of the candles, Barry surveyed the room. The fire blazed merrily, the candles flickered, offering a suffused golden glow to the room.

Romantic. Very romantic and perfect for what he had in mind.

Satisfied, he began to remove his clothes, remembering the small blue box in the pocket of his trousers. Pulling it out, he palmed it as he looked at Mel sleeping naked on the bed. Kissing it, he placed it under the pillow.

Then, after he finished undressing, he climbed onto the bed, taking care not to wake her. God, he was tired. Twenty-four hours since he'd last slept and he was desperate to close his eyes. But if everything went well, he could sleep tomorrow. So could Mel for that matter. Right beside him. As his wife. Just as it should be.

He inhaled the soft blend of her natural scent—lemon with a hint of something else, something mysterious, sexy. Something that turned him on every time he caught the slightest whiff.

Picking up the pink rose off her pillow where he'd placed it, he stroked it over her neck, dragging the velvety petals down lower into the valley between her breasts. A small wriggle and a muffled grunt were the only indication that anything was penetrating her heavy slumber.

Leaning down, he licked around a nipple, running his tongue in smaller and smaller circles until just the tip was left. Enclosing it in his mouth, he relished the taste and feel of it and suckled on it gently, light tugs intended to arouse rather than awaken, as he circled the other with his fingertip.

She squirmed more, biting her lip in her sleep as a little moan hummed free.

He was desperate for her, to hear her plead with him, beg him for more.

A dark thought taunted him, the image of her between her two lovers, screaming their names. Anger surged through him, making him want to lash out.

Why, Melissa, why?

He shook his head as if to shake the thoughts from it. No, no going down that path. When she woke, he would forgive her. She would have to be punished...later, but that was his right. She was his. She would always be his. She knew that. He knew she did.

The taunting sight of her naked body stretched out under him sent a surge of need through him. So many nights he'd dreamed of this, taking her like this. He would not spoil it. Not now. Tonight was about pleasure, for both of them.

Moving down the bed, Barry positioned himself between her legs, dragging the rose down over her skin in circular trails. The smell that greeted him made his cock stiff, its length growing longer until the skin was stretched tight.

As much as he would have loved Melissa to take him into the delicious heat of her mouth, he wasn't prepared to trust her desire not to do him a serious injury with her teeth until he'd had a chance to explain.

Instead he trailed the rose up her inner thighs from her knee to the damp lips of her pussy. She'd shaved there, but he didn't mind. In fact, he liked it. He grinned as her hips made a small involuntary jerk upward in time with the caress of the rosebud. When he noticed her breath coming in shorter little puffs, her body twisting as if searching for satisfaction, he put the rose down and braced his hands on either side of her hips as watched her juices start leaking from her pussy.

His head lifted as she whispered something. She was still halfway between sleeping and waking, just how he wanted her.

Running his finger through the juices gathering on the swollen lips of her sex, he eased a finger inside, thrusting gently, a second one joining the first. When her breathing escalated further, the wetness spilling onto his fingers, he curled a finger up, manipulating her G-spot. Leaning over her, he took a nipple into his mouth again.

He hid a small smile when she came awake and opened her eyes.

"Hello, sweetness."

"*Barry?* What—"

The moment she realized she couldn't move, her expression changed. Surprise turned to shock, changed to anger. That fire of hers he loved so much surged to the fore. She tugged on the leather bands that tied her wrists to the headboard. Yanked on the ankle restraints keeping her spread-eagled, her pussy open to his ministrations. Watching her struggle only made him harder, his cock throb.

"Barry! Let me go, you bastard!" she yelled, and wriggled with more determination, pulling and groaning. "Don't you dare."

He released her nipple with a pop. Pulled his fingers back to a gentle in and out. "You know, Mel, I've always thought that if two people are in love, that trust plays a big part of their relationship. That's essential for a happy marriage, wouldn't you agree?"

"What the hell are you talking about? Let me go! You have no fucking right. Let me go *now*!"

He ignored the escalation of her temper and carried on. "It really comes down to communication. The man and the woman need to talk, yes?"

"*Barry*. Let. Me. Go."

"You and I needed to talk. Alone. So here we are." He flicked a nipple with his finger.

"Don't do this, Barry. It won't solve anything." Her voice was becoming desperate.

"No? I think things are going very well. At least I have your undivided attention now, don't I?" Reaching behind him, he retrieved the dildo and held it up for her to see. Keeping his face serious, although it was hard when her body was reacting so beautifully, he slowly inserted the dildo into her cunt. Her body went taut. "Feel good?"

"No."

"Oh, but it will, Mel. Now where was I? Oh, that's right. Communication. Take something like this for example…"

Raising himself onto his knees, he reached to the bedside table for the piece of paper he'd left there and held it up.

Melissa stilled and narrowed her eyes, straining to see. "What is it?"

"It says that I'm getting married. To you. Wonderful, yes?"

Her face was becoming flushed with her struggles. "No. You call that communication? You *telling* me we're getting married? Please, Barry. Untie me. Let me go."

Her eyes clouded and began to water, and he felt a moment's hesitation about what he was doing.

No. He had to do this. It was the only way to make her realize.

"We were meant to be, sweetness. You realize that, don't you? Say yes. Let's get married here. I've made the arrangements already. We can return to Sydney as husband and wife."

"But I don't love you," she gritted out.

"Love is not something you can just turn off like a tap," he snapped. "You love me. I know you do. You were scared, I understand that," he added softly. "But we have time, Melissa. All the time in the world."

Reaching under the pillow, he retrieved the small box. Flicking the lid, he looked at the exquisite solitaire diamond that lay nestled in the blue velvet. He turned it around to show her.

"Beautiful, isn't it? Not as beautiful as the lady it's intended for, though. I bought you a new one. This will be a fresh start for us, Mel. I want everything to be perfect."

He reached for her finger, working the other ring she was wearing off. He tossed it over his shoulder. "You certainly won't be needing that piece of crap anymore."

She whimpered and he noted she'd redoubled her efforts to get free. He sighed. This was going to take longer than he thought. She was apparently quite determined to be difficult. He put the ring aside.

He leaned over to brush a kiss on her forehead, feeling her body stiffen under his. "There hasn't been another woman for me since you. I love you, Mel. So much. Too much to let you go."

"I don't want to hear it," she ground out. "I don't want to marry you. Let me go, Barry, or I'll scream."

He became angry. "No! You think you can call for your *lovers* and they'll come running?" he yelled. "No one will hear you. You've put me through hell, Mel. Nearly sent me out of my mind searching for you."

He paused when her struggles ceased abruptly, conscious of how his voice had risen. He took a deep breath to bring his racing pulse under control.

"It's sad too because I really can't live without you. Not for another minute. So I guess I'll just have to keep you tied up until you say yes."

He moved into position between her legs, lowering himself until his body blanketed hers, held in the cradle of her hips.

"I love you, Mel. My heart is yours. Only yours. Please, I don't want to fight with you anymore, but I don't know what else I can do…"

He cupped her face in his hands, kissing her, ignoring the feel of her stiffening underneath him as he drowned in the feel and smell of her. Until the thought that she had nearly escaped him again made him realize all he would lose if he lost her.

Overcome by the love he felt, he kissed her harder.

A soft swishing sound made him pause. His head lifted as the overhead lights blasted the room into brightness and the bedroom door slammed open to bang against the wall.

"Noooooo!" he roared, and slipped a hand under the pillow, pulling out his last defense.

In that instant when he caught sight of Melissa bound and restrained on the bed, Barry lying on top of her naked, Alex's breath jammed to a stop in his throat and a hate stronger, darker, colder than he'd ever felt before flooded through him like a tidal wave. His vision went red and he wanted to kill.

Only Richard's roar beside him, a sound of such primal, incandescent rage, and his movement as he stood, jerked Alex out of his momentary stasis. That and the light shining on the ugly gray barrel of a gun as Barry whipped it around to point at the easy target Richard presented.

Instinct took over and Alex dived for Richard, knocking them both to the floor. The room erupted. Loud bangs. Screaming.

Searing pain filled his chest and he gasped once before darkness filled his vision and the noises faded…

Chapter Nine

Richard leaned against the wall.

From where he stood, he could watch Alex as well as Melissa as she slept, her head resting on Alex's hospital bed, her fingers entwined with his.

She'd rallied amazingly well after the incident with Barry. Apart from trying to tear her ex's head off once they released her from the bindings Barry had placed on her. But the rage was good—and they'd arrived before Barry could actually rape her. Five minutes later... Shit! Too close.

Richard rubbed a closed fist against the hard knot lodged in his chest. In the week since Barry had been taken out, he felt as though he hadn't been able to take a single decent breath around the tightness. It was nothing compared to what Alex had gone through. He was still coming to terms with the fact that Alex had nearly died because of him.

The minute they'd burst into that house and he'd seen Melissa—terrified, bound and spread out on that bed, Barry naked on top of her—his worst nightmares had become reality. All those years of training...all gone as if they'd never been. Just the suffocating fury. The choking rage to kill.

Alex had kept his cool. Always. Richard absently rotated his shoulder to relieve the ache from landing on it when Alex crashed into him. Bits and pieces were coming back to him, more details—Alex barreling into him like a battering ram to push him out of the way as Barry raised his gun. Melissa screaming.

Alex's last words before the bullet that tore through his chest knocked him out...

He closed his eyes briefly against that image. It should be him lying on the bed, fighting for his life — not Alex.

With concern, he watched his best friend, the uneven rise and fall of his chest, his face pale. And Melissa... Pain filled Richard and he turned to the window, looking out at the gray day outside.

He'd nearly lost both of them. It should have been him. Dammit! Why did Alex have to be such a fucking hero? He wanted to hit something. Rant. Yell.

What a bloody mess. His head dropped down and he squeezed his eyes shut, forcing the moisture back.

A small hand landed on his shoulder, another on his arm, and he placed his hand over Melissa's.

"He'll be okay, Rich. We all will."

"Sure we will." He patted her hand.

"Have I said thank you?"

"For what?"

"For saving me. If you and Alex—"

"No, puss. Alex saved you."

He turned around. Just looking at her, the worry in her eyes for Alex, made his heart clench. Alex loved her — hell, the man was head over heels. And it wasn't hard to see how much Melissa loved Alex. She hadn't left his side for more than a few minutes since they brought him out of surgery.

Richard may have been slow admitting it, but he loved Melissa too. Everything about her. Her smell. Her laugh. The way her eyes lit up when she was having fun with him. Her touches...

Hands cupping her face, he lowered his head and kissed her. Slow, storing the feel and taste away, enough to last him a lifetime if necessary. Forever. When he finally lifted his head, pulled back enough to sear her image into his mind, her cheeks were wet.

"I love you, Melissa. Always—"

"Hey," a deep voice croaked from the bed.

Melissa spun around and shot out of his arms, rushing over to the bed. "Alex!"

The irony of the moment wasn't lost on him. For the first time in a long time, he'd actually let those three words out of his mouth and the woman hadn't even noticed.

Richard followed her, chest tight as he watched Melissa cover Alex's face and mouth with kisses, her soft, "I love you, you big lug," bringing a slow, wide smile to Alex's face.

In spite of the fact that Richard was finally able to take a deep breath again, he recognized the moment for what it was, and the hurt seared him.

He smiled though and gripped Alex's outstretched hand. "Alex. You made it."

"*We* did."

Yes, they had. The two people he loved most in the world were going to be all right. They'd be good together. Alex needed Melissa more than he'd ever admit. She gave his life lightness. Stupid bugger was too bloody serious by half. And Melissa… God, her love for Alex was shining all over her sweet face.

"Richard?" Alex asked, a frown creasing his forehead.

Richard shook off the melancholy taking over him and pasted the smile back on his face. "You had us worried. Poor Melissa aged ten years watching over you."

"Why, you!" Melissa turned and whacked him playfully on the arm. "Are you inferring I look like an old hag?"

"No, puss, you look beautiful as always." He looked back at Alex and the next words stuck in his throat. He coughed, trying to clear the lump. "But I'll leave you in Melissa's tender care for now, mate. I have a few things to…do. Thanks, Alex. For everything."

"Richard?" Alex struggled to rise until Melissa stopped him. "Don't—" Alex gasped as he flopped back onto the bed, a grimace crossing his features.

Melissa smoothed a hand over Alex's brow. "Take it easy, Alex. Richard will be back soon." She turned to face him, smiling, confident now that Alex was awake. "Won't you?"

"Sure, I'll be around."

Wrapping a hand around her neck, he placed a fleeting kiss on Melissa's brow then grasped Alex's hand tightly once more, ignoring the questioning look his friend threw him before turning and leaving the hospital.

* * * * *

The past couple of weeks caught up with Melissa. Tired of the endless worry—over Barry then Alex, and now the missing Richard—Melissa leaned back against the tiles in her shower, letting the hot water flow over her and shut her eyes.

Since Richard had walked out of the hospital that day a week ago, Alex had become quiet, withdrawn, agitated, as if he couldn't wait to get out of there. And in spite of his repeated "Nothing…nothing" and a pat on her hand whenever she asked what was wrong, it was fucking obvious it was a pretty big *something* he had on his mind.

No contact from Richard. Not answering his phone or the SMSs she'd sent. And now Alex was due to be discharged and that was apparently that. She'd begun to feel she'd overstayed her welcome at the hospital.

Which had made her face the thing that had been bothering *her*.

It wasn't as if the three of them had talked about "after". And upon reflection, something she'd done again and again the past week, apart from all the "you're ours" assertions while they were fucking her—something she now wrote off to heat-of-the-moment-in-the-middle-of-hot-sex—the fact was that there'd been no words of forever, or even after. At best it could be called an affair. Intense. Full of the most amazing, satisfying sex any woman could ask for. Highly emotional. But apparently an affair, nonetheless.

Which just sucked for her. She felt anger flare. Anger at herself, not Richard or Alex. Could she be any more stupid? Falling in love with two men, for God's sake! And it was no use denying it—she was way beyond infatuation or simple lust. This was love—no illusions there. She banged a clenched fist on the tiled wall of the shower in frustration.

What tore at her was that after the uncertainty of the last week she was no longer under any illusions that Richard or Alex felt the same way.

Almost desperate for any word on Richard, she'd spent last night on the internet.

Bad move. Richard's lovers over the past twelve months—with the exception of herself—read like a who's who of the rich and beautiful in London. Hell, now that she was safe, he'd probably already gone back to the fan club.

At that thought her eyes watered again and she wiped angrily at them. It seemed as though she'd been doing nothing but crying lately. If nothing else she'd been forced to face the stupid fantasy she'd allowed herself to be lulled into. A fantasy their continued presence hadn't allowed her to face the reality of until now, when she was finally left alone.

She ran the soap over her body, seeing first Alex then Richard in her mind's eye. With a growl, she stomped on the images. No, she couldn't go there. The hurt was too strong, too fresh. Swallowing down on a sob that felt as if a watermelon had lodged in her throat, she flicked off the shower, pulling the rope of her hair around to the front and twisting the water out of it before she slid open the glass screen.

She gasped when she saw Richard there, leaning against the wall. Jeans hugging his hips, the top button undone, and no shirt... Never fully quenched, the hunger for him rose again. God, she'd missed him so much.

His brow was furrowed, his blue eyes stormy.

But after what had happened, she felt on rocky ground, unsure what to do, to say. Instead she said nothing and grabbed for a towel, but Richard reached out and caught the other end.

"I swear, Melissa, if I see that look in your eyes again, I'm going to... Hell, puss, come here!"

Tugging on the towel, he pulled her over to him, wrapping an arm around her waist.

"You'll get wet..."

"I don't fucking care, do I? I was going to join you. In fact, I started to undress, intending to do just that, but I decided to watch you instead." His voice softened as he ran a hand over her hair, looking at her intently. "I could watch you for hours, love, and never grow bored. You're so beautiful—"

Her eyes flashed at him as anger, bred from her disappointment at his desertion, his rejection, flamed inside her. "No, I'm not. I wish you'd stop talking such bloody nonsense." She wrenched out of his arms. "You must think I'm so stupid." She thought back to her little foray on the internet. "God, you date models, for heaven's sake, Rich. Heiresses. Like Annabelle-fucking-Dunleavy...except without the farting problem, I'm sure."

Richard bellowed and laughed out loud, and it smoothed the dark shadows away from his eyes. No wonder his ladies all loved him—the only man who came close to him in looks was Alex. And when Richard smiled like this...

"No, no farting allowed."

His laughter petered out and an unsettling look, purely male and full of proprietary satisfaction, filled his eyes. "Ah puss, you've been checking up on me?"

God, male ego—was any man immune to it? And so what the hell if she had?

In a huff, she wrapped the towel around her, tucked the end in between her breasts and made to brush past him. "All gorgeous women I can't even begin to compete with. Look, thank you for your help with Barry, but why don't you just go, Rich. I'm sure at least one of your ladies is calling your name."

Hooking an arm around her waist, he brought her back to him, his frown returning as he pulled her flush against his body. "Compete?" He laughed, unlike before, the sound abrupt and cold. "You're crazy. There is no bloody competition."

The harshness of his reply felt like a slap in the face to her already shaky self-esteem. Her heart plummeted to her feet and she felt cold all over. "Well, I guess that puts me in my place. Thanks." She pushed against him, breaking out of his hold. What she needed was to get away from him. Now that she knew where she stood with him, it was killing her to have him so close and know that this was all it was—a sexual attraction. Nothing more, nothing less. *Fuck buddies*, in spite of what he'd told her once. Friends with benefits.

But it wasn't enough. After what she'd shared with Richard and Alex, it would never be enough.

Rough hands grabbed her from behind, spinning her around. "No. Hang on a minute. Dammit, Melissa! Yes, I have dated some beautiful women, I won't deny that, but none of them made me feel the way you do…"

She tried to look away from the intense blue of his eyes, eyes now sparkling with icy shards as if in anger. His arms held hers pinned against her sides and he shook her. "Look at me, damn you!"

The fierceness of his expression made her knees tremble.

"None of them make me feel as if I'll die if I can't touch them. Or like how just a smile makes me feel as though I'm the luckiest man in the world." He grabbed her chin roughly and forced her gaze to his. "And none of them makes me feel…" he flicked a thumb over her bottom lip, "Christ, puss…like I'd be fucking lost without them." The final words came out as almost a growl and lowering his head, he covered her mouth with his, all gentleness gone, eating at her lips hungrily until she fought to breathe.

When he finally held her away from him, they were both panting and breathless.

"That's how you make me feel, Melissa." He loosened his hold on her, reaching down to pick up her hand, laying it against his chest where she could feel the rapid pounding of his heart.

"Now before I lose control and fuck you up against the wall, come with me—I brought breakfast."

He frowned when her stomach rumbled in response to the tantalizing smells that met her nose at the breakfast nook. He'd taken a few minutes to lay it all out, napkins and all. But from the look of her, and her stomach's reaction, she hadn't been eating— Bugger it, he knew it! Well, she could eat, but breakfast wasn't all he'd brought.

Richard watched impatiently as Melissa sipped her juice, eyeing the small bundle wrapped in the linen napkin in front of her.

She parted the loose knot on the napkin, the corners falling apart to reveal the rich, buttery croissant within. He couldn't stifle the pleased grin when her eyes widened as she picked up the delicate antique emerald and diamond necklace draped over it. Her mouth dropped open as she looked from him to the elaborate strands of gems she held so nervously in her fingers.

"The emeralds always remind me of you, love—same color as your beautiful eyes."

"But...but..." was all Melissa could manage to say.

"Oh and in case you're wondering, yes, that piece is part of the family jewels. So don't lose it, okay?"

He nodded at the card that lay partly hidden beneath the flaky pastry.

"Read it," he commanded, his voice gruff in response to the emotion swirling between them.

He watched as she swallowed. Melissa would never be considered a classic beauty, but at that moment, he'd never seen a more adorable, sexy sight in his life—hair damp, luscious body wrapped in nothing but a towel, face flushed... It was a sight he intended to wake up to every morning for the rest of his life.

"To the woman who is more beautiful, more precious to me..." she paused briefly as she hitched a breath, "than the finest jewels." Melissa looked up at him, green eyes swimming with tears. When she smiled, that adorable smile with the little dimple, a solitary tear slid over her lid and down her cheek. His heart nearly stopped beating. Was it possible she really didn't have a clue the effect she had on him?

He stood and moved around behind her, taking the necklace from her hand and undoing the fiddly little clasp while she moved the long fall of damp hair to the side. He hooked the clasp closed, watching as the pear-shaped diamond settled at the top of her cleavage, and placed a long kiss on her neck.

Crouching beside her, he waited while she turned in her seat until she faced him. "I'm not great with the words, puss...but I love you, Melissa Blake. Just you. Always and forever." He reached up to kiss her, pulling her toward him until he could cover her mouth with his, twining his tongue with hers, trying to show her how much he'd missed her. When she rubbed her tongue alongside his, he groaned, kissing her harder. She was laughing and breathless when he moved back.

"For a man who isn't 'great with the words', Richard Danville, you're doing a wonderful job."

"Good. Just don't forget it. Now let's eat. I'm starved."

Richard watched Melissa closely as she tried to eat. She'd lost a few pounds, her face especially was looking a little thinner than before. He didn't want her losing weight. He loved her exactly the way she was—all curves and softness. Womanly. Feminine.

After watching her pick at the first croissant, the minute she finished it, he rose, went to the oven and removed another one. "Eat," he said as he placed it on her plate.

"I'm full."

"You're not. You can't be. You haven't eaten enough to feed a sparrow. Eat that while I fill you in."

Melissa paused with her knife in her hand. "Fill me in? Well, yes, that would be nice. Where have you been? I was…worried."

A hand wrapped around her neck, Richard reached across the table to kiss her again.

After a few delicious moments, he pulled away. "No, you were hurt. You thought I'd left you, didn't you?"

"What was I supposed to think?"

Richard placed his hand over Melissa's. "You were supposed to have a little faith, puss." Richard picked up his cup of tea and took a sip. "I had to go get my head out of my arse. It was plugged up there so tight, it took some doing."

Picking up her hand, he caressed it, his eyes focused on her fingers.

"I owe you an explanation." He lifted his eyes to look at her briefly. This was it, what he'd been dreading. But he had to tell her. She had to know before they could go forward. But even though the small chance was there that she'd be like Cilla, it was a chance he had to take. For all of them.

"About seven years ago I was engaged. To a lovely girl called Lanie." Richard gave her a sad smile. "Back then I wasn't like the Richard you met. Lanie and I were head over heels about each other. I never looked at any other women—she was my life, Melissa. Any leave I had from the unit, I'd be straight back to Lanie. We'd stay bundled up in her flat for every second we could grab.

Richard lifted her hand until she rose from her seat. "Come here, love." Tugging on her hand until she stood in front of him, he pulled her down onto his lap. He wrapped his arms around her waist as she settled against him. "One leave we'd been out to dinner at the local pub. Walking home, we were attacked by three young men. One of whom was armed. Two of them restrained me while the one with the gun held it to Lanie's head. I tried to reason with him, but seeing her in danger... I lost it. In the ensuing tussle she was accidentally killed. It was instant, that's the only consolation I have."

"God, no! Oh, Richard." Melissa's arms tightened around his neck as she hugged him.

His voice lowered. "I went into a very dark period after that. Took me a long time to get over it. That was when Alex and I first started sharing women. Not all the time, but something changed in me with Lanie's death, Melissa. The only way I could get close, emotionally close to a woman, was when I was sharing her. Until Cilla."

"Alex's wife?" Melissa's eyebrows rose.

"I guess Alex never told you about that part."

"No."

"In the beginning it was like Alex and I share with you. We both fell for her. We thought she felt the same way about us. That she wanted both of us. It wasn't until later, after Alex married her, we found out that actually she couldn't stand me—she'd really wanted just Alex. The whole thing blew up about six months into the marriage. After a lot of fights, a lot of hurt, I moved out. But the damage with Alex and Cilla had been done. When Alex divorced her...let's just say it was nasty.

"After that though, I pulled away from all women emotionally. Until you. You got under my skin, puss. And I can't get you out. I don't want you out."

"I love you, Richard. That's why I was so upset when you disappeared." Melissa started to cry, unable to stop the cascade of tears. "I think you're the one who needs the speech about having a little faith, Rich."

He ducked his head—she had him there.

"So why did you go away?" she asked. "Did you think I didn't love you?" She looked shocked as a thought occurred to her. "God, you didn't think that I only wanted Alex, did you?"

"It may have crossed my mind."

"Thought so. You bloody idiot!"

"It wasn't just that. I was responsible for protecting you, Melissa. And even though you're fine now, you're safe, I still felt like I'd failed—again."

"But you didn't. Like you said, I'm fine. Barry's in jail."

"Thank God." Richard hugged her tighter, unable to speak for long moments.

"I was first in the room where Barry was holding you."

"Yes."

"What I saw when I burst through that door… You tied and bound. Barry…"

"Yes, I remember."

"And the look on your face, love…well…I was ready to rip Barry apart with my bare hands if necessary. Barry had a gun. I saw it, but I didn't care. My only focus was getting to you."

"So Alex pushed you out of the way. He took the bullet Barry meant for you."

"He did. And see, I felt as though I'd failed both of you."

"But that's crazy. You would have done the same for him."

"I would. But in my mind, seeing you like that, it was Lanie all over again."

He kissed her softly.

"I love you, Melissa."

"And I love you. And Alex too. As much as I love you, Rich. I don't ever want to have to choose. I don't think I could."

Relief filled him. Happiness too. "You won't have to. You're marrying both of us."

"But how?"

"I have a plan. We can work out the fine details later. But you belong to both of us, puss. Be quite clear on that." He cradled her face in his hand. "Just as we belong to you. If you're sure that's what you want..."

"Yes, I'm sure! But what about your family? Your friends?"

"My parents are beyond shocking. They've already been through this once with me, remember?

"My mother's thrilled. I went home after I left the hospital. I needed someone to talk it out with, and I told her all about you—about the three of us." He tucked a finger under her necklace, running his finger along the elaborate setting of diamonds and emeralds. "This was hers, you know," he said. "It's given to the wife of the eldest Danville son in every generation. When I told her I was coming back to get you, she had it cleaned so I could give it to you if you said yes."

"But you haven't asked me."

He laughed. "Cocky bastard, aren't I?"

Melissa smiled. "I guess I can live with it. Somebody has to."

The laughter stopped, but the smile remained. "So, Melissa Blake, will you marry me and Alex, and live happily ever after with us?"

"Yes, you goof. You know I will."

"Thought so. Now go and get dressed so we can pick Alex up from the hospital. After being without you for a week, I have plans for the three of us and they all involve being naked—or mostly so."

He kissed her once more then they both stood. "I'll clean up here. I want you to pack a bag too. Enough for a week. I'm guessing, though," Richard grinned and leaned over her, licking a small flake of pastry off her cheek before he kissed her quickly, "you're going to be naked about one minute after Alex gets you home."

"But what—"

"Dress! I'll fill you in, in the car on the way. You need to call Cynthia? No, don't answer that—I'll call her. Go. Go! And pack something slinky and sexy. You're getting married, remember?"

Richard had just finished putting the plates away when he had the feeling he was being watched. He turned around and almost jumped out of his skin at the sight of Alex standing in the doorway to the living room. The little adrenaline surge hit him hard. "Shit, where the hell did you come from?"

"More importantly, where the hell did you *go*?"

"To sort things out. Which I did. And I'm back. For good, this time."

A big smile creased Alex's face. "No more running?"

"No, and I've told Melissa everything."

"That's good to hear." He hugged Richard, slapping him on the back. "Damn good."

"Melissa and I were going to come and get you. How did you get here?"

"Cab. Checked myself out. I've been worried—"

A squeal from the direction of the bedroom made them both turn. "Alex!" said Melissa, rushing over to him. She wrapped her arms around his neck, kissing his face and making him laugh.

"That's some welcome, baby. A guy could get used to it."

When she finally let go, Richard tucked her back to his front with an arm around her waist.

"Didn't get very far, hey, puss?" he murmured into her ear.

"What—"

She looked down and blushed. "Ooops!"

"Don't get dressed on my account, baby," said Alex, his eyes full of admiration and a healthy dose of lust at Melissa's naked state. His attention locked onto Melissa's chest though, and he whistled and grinned at Richard. "The Danville family jewels, no less. Does this mean what I think it means?"

"It does. It means we—the three of us—are making this permanent. I've asked Melissa on behalf of both of us and she said yes."

"About bloody time, Richard. I was beginning to wonder when and if you'd come to your senses."

* * * * *

The next day
Gardens of Anderleigh House, Derbeyshire, seat of the Danvilles

"A bride shouldn't be standing alone on her wedding day, Mrs. Danville."

Melissa turned at Lizzy's voice beside her. She automatically looked around for Tom, who seemed to never be more than a breath away from his heavily pregnant wife. He formed part of the masculine huddle comprising Richard, Alex and Richard's father, about fifteen feet away. More than a breath, but his eyes watched his wife closely just the same in spite of the conversation he was meant to be a participant of. Melissa had no doubt that if Elizabeth so much as sneezed, Tom would be beside her before she could open her eyes. "Not quite Mrs. Danville yet," Melissa corrected with a soft smile. "Not until next month anyway." The "legal" wedding, for

Richard and her, was booked for then. At Alex's prompting, she would take Richard's name.

"Rubbish." Lizzy waved her hand. "I have a feeling you'll always consider this as the day you were married, Mel. Irrespective of what date the official marriage license says.

"You're right, you know." Melissa beamed at her, unable to hide her happiness at being "married" to both Richard and Alex. Richard had organized everything, including a celebrant to oversee their "commitment" ceremony and a very intimate selection of friends and family to witness it. "I know, I can't stop grinning like a big kid. But I'm so happy, Lizzy."

"And so are Richard and Alex—it's pretty obvious how much they both love you, Melissa." Lizzy tucked her hand inside Melissa's elbow. "I already like Alex and I'm sure I'll grow to love him over the years since he's a part of the two of you, but I'm especially happy for you and Richard. He really needs this, Melissa. He needs you."

"I know." Melissa could feel herself getting teary again. It was why she'd grabbed a moment alone while she could.

"They better be happy tears, or Richard will have my head on a platter."

"Oh, they're happy all right. What girl wouldn't want to be in my position?"

Also by Susie Charles

Velvet Strokes
Were Watching 1: Candid Camera
Were Watching 2: Hanging By a Moment

About the Author

One thing Susie Charles could never say is that her life has been boring. Having lived in more places than she can remember and tried enough different occupations to fill a job guide, has given her a wealth of experiences to draw upon in her stories.

Now, as a writer of erotic romances, she works diligently to live up to her lusty image. Always looking for inspiration wherever she can find it, she has a disconcerting habit of checking out the "talent" when she goes shopping with her adult daughters—although, for them, she draws the line at whistling at strange men. She spends her spare time walking along the beach where she lives, ostensibly exercising while she plans new stories, but more often than not visually distracted by the delicious abundance of almost naked male flesh she uses as "inspiration".

Needless to say, with her boundless and undiminished appreciation for the male of the species, her heroes are always hunky sex gods who will do *anything* to make their lady happy. Being of the curvy variety herself and knowing how most males just love curves, her heroines are never model-thin, and are fun, sassy and intelligent to boot.

Susie welcomes comments from readers. You can find her website and email address on her author bio page at www.ellorascave.com.

Tell Us What You Think

We appreciate hearing reader opinions about our books. You can email us at Comments@EllorasCave.com.

Why an electronic book?

We live in the Information Age—an exciting time in the history of human civilization, in which technology rules supreme and continues to progress in leaps and bounds every minute of every day. For a multitude of reasons, more and more avid literary fans are opting to purchase e-books instead of paper books. The question from those not yet initiated into the world of electronic reading is simply: *Why?*

1. *Price.* An electronic title at Ellora's Cave Publishing and Cerridwen Press runs anywhere from 40% to 75% less than the cover price of the exact same title in paperback format. Why? Basic mathematics and cost. It is less expensive to publish an e-book (no paper and printing, no warehousing and shipping) than it is to publish a paperback, so the savings are passed along to the consumer.

2. *Space.* Running out of room in your house for your books? That is one worry you will never have with electronic books. For a low one-time cost, you can purchase a handheld device specifically designed for e-reading. Many e-readers have large, convenient screens for viewing. Better yet, hundreds of titles can be stored within your new library—on a single microchip. There are a variety of e-readers from different manufacturers. You can also read e-books on your PC or laptop computer. (Please note that Ellora's Cave does not endorse any specific brands.

You can check our websites at www.ellorascave.com or www.cerridwenpress.com for information we make available to new consumers.)

3. *Mobility.* Because your new e-library consists of only a microchip within a small, easily transportable e-reader, your entire cache of books can be taken with you wherever you go.

4. *Personal Viewing Preferences.* Are the words you are currently reading too small? Too large? Too… ANNOYING? Paperback books cannot be modified according to personal preferences, but e-books can.

5. *Instant Gratification.* Is it the middle of the night and all the bookstores near you are closed? Are you tired of waiting days, sometimes weeks, for bookstores to ship the novels you bought? Ellora's Cave Publishing sells instantaneous downloads twenty-four hours a day, seven days a week, every day of the year. Our webstore is never closed. Our e-book delivery system is 100% automated, meaning your order is filled as soon as you pay for it.

Those are a few of the top reasons why electronic books are replacing paperbacks for many avid readers.

As always, Ellora's Cave and Cerridwen Press welcome your questions and comments. We invite you to email us at Comments@ellorascave.com or write to us directly at Ellora's Cave Publishing Inc., 1056 Home Avenue, Akron, OH 44310-3502.

COMING TO A BOOKSTORE NEAR YOU!

ELLORA'S CAVE

Bestselling Authors Tour

UPDATES AVAILABLE AT
WWW.ELLORASCAVE.COM

Discover for yourself why readers can't get enough of the multiple award-winning publisher
Ellora's Cave.
Whether you prefer e-books or paperbacks,
be sure to visit EC on the web at
www.ellorascave.com
for an erotic reading experience that will leave you breathless.

Printed in Great Britain by
Amazon.co.uk, Ltd.,
Marston Gate.